Some Tulip

Lydia Coulter

Coulter Publishing

Some Tulip

First published in Great Britain in 2024 by Lydia Coulter

Copyright © 2024 by Lydia Coulter

The right of Lydia Coulter to be identified as the author of this work has been asserted in accordance with the Copyright, Designs and Patents Act 1988.

A CIP catalogue record for this book is available from the British Library.

ISBN 978-1-0369-0009-0

Printed and bound in Great Britain by CPI Printing

Lydia Coulter

86-90 Paul Street

London, EC2A 4NE

lydiacoulter.com

Contents

Tulip/ˈtjuːlɪp/ *noun*

Slang: A playful term used to describe someone who is acting foolish or a bit stupid, often in a light-hearted or affectionate manner. Example: "Ah, you're some tulip for forgetting your keys again!"

Chapter One

There was a Sarah-shaped hole in the wedding party, which Aoife and Morag only discovered five hours after the bride-to-be had vanished.

"Sarah, Sarah," Morag half-whispered as she tapped on the door. "Come on now, let us in."

They'd been standing barefoot in the corridor for fifteen minutes, their pedicured toes curling against the plush carpet, while Morag insisted on attempting to quietly wake up a woman who was known for sleeping like the dead. A ludicrous endeavour in Aoife's eyes; there was one thing and one thing only Sarah responded to in a deep sleep – noise so loud and obnoxious it could wake the saints.

"I don't want to wake everybody up," Morag protested, despite the fact that the hotel was overrun with guests for that very wedding.

"Cop onto yourself now, Morag," Aoife urged, her patience wearing thin. "They're going to be awake in half an hour anyway. And if we don't wake her up – they'll be waiting even longer…"

"I am *not* going to be the one telling half the hotel we couldn't get the bride out of bed on the morning of her own wedding. The shame of it!"

Shame, shame. Riddled with unresolved shame and Catholic guilt to the point where they were stood outside of the bridal suite like two eejits trying to sell pork sausages to vegans, because one of them felt too ashamed to be heard and let into a place where they needed to be if this wedding was to take place at all.

You could say the Catholics were well ahead of cancel culture in that they were already sorry for everything they'd ever done, often before they'd even done it. The proof was in this very pudding.

"We'll still be here waking her up when the priest arrives if you keep fannying on like this." Aoife took her turn and planted herself in front of the door.

With a small but mighty fist, she rapped loudly on the teak-stained wood. Morag flinched. "Here now, Sarah, wake up and let us in. You've a big hunk of a fella downstairs waiting to perform a miracle and make an honest woman of you."

Morag rolled her eyes. She rolled them so hard that, for a second, Aoife thought she might go blind.

"Are ye actually going to continue or just stare into space like a cow looking at a passing train?"

"Right, yes." Aoife knocked again. "Open up now you daft mare, your girl is thirsty. You've got the breakfast in there and I'm fucking starving. Let's get this show on the road before we all die of old age."

"Do you need to be so loud?" Morag hissed.

"Loud? There are six bottles of champagne and a breakfast spread in there, Morag – I need to be louder."

"Maybe she's in with Chris?"

"On the morning of the wedding? Behave. Do you think they'd piss tradition up the wall after flying Father O'Connor all the way from Cork to Crete? The man's probably still got jetlag and a sunburn to boot."

"Poor bloke, I've never seen anybody sweat so much." Morag paused. "You know, I caught him around the pool yesterday trying to get an impromptu Mass going by the bar... Now there's an altar I'd pray at.

Here, why don't you go down to Reception and shake your arse at yer man yesterday who was ogling you like you were the Second Coming? He'll let us in."

"Morag, are you suggesting I seduce a man who'd have my poor dear mother turning in her grave?"

"Yer ma's not dead, Aoife. And this is important – so yes, I am insisting you go and shake your bits at the bloke so we can get to the other side of that door."

Aoife paused for a moment as if to object, but only because she wished she'd thought of weaponising her talent for flirting first. She soon left with a grimace and returned ten minutes later with a look of benign satisfaction and a greasy pole of a man trotting eagerly behind like a puppy promised a treat. And all it took, she thought, was the mere insinuation that there might be five minutes' heavy petting later that evening.

He wanted a shift but by God, he wouldn't be getting one no matter how much she'd had to drink. She realised, more than anyone, that she'd done some dicey things with sketchy men in her thirty-eight years, but the man had more grease in his hair than a car engine.

Then again, never say never. She'd already had a once-over at the groomsmen and decided her fortunes best lay elsewhere.

At least it wouldn't be as bad as the time she slept with a bloke on holiday in Bulgaria and woke up to find he had no teeth. She'd never moved so fast. She got back to her own room to find she had her knickers on backwards and her left boob in the lobby downstairs asking what time breakfast started.

Stavros placed his hands gingerly on Aoife's waist and moved her to the side. Morag caught the startled look on her friend's face as she tingled in places she had hoped she wouldn't.

There was a purposeful twitch in his biceps as he withdrew the key-card from the whirring lock and slowly placed it back in his pocket.

"If you need me... you know where I am," he said to Aoife, and only Aoife, before he strode down the corridor, the sharp click of his patent brogues growing ever fainter.

She – whose gaze had inadvertently followed the Greek until he disappeared from view – turned back to Morag, who stared with an impatiently indignant look and firmly grasped the handle of the door. The woman made a beeline for the curtains and drenched the crisp white hotel room in bright morning light.

She turned to find Aoife standing open-mouthed at the undisturbed bed in the adjacent room.

"Where the fuck has she got to?" she asked, her voice a mix of confusion and dawning horror.

"Morag – do you have your phone? Ring her," Aoife said, pulling her own from her robe and beginning to jab the glass screen with desperation.

"Maybe she's gone for a walk?" Morag said, her voice rising.

"The woman who gets a taxi to cross the road going for a walk on the morning of her wedding?" Aoife said with the phone to her ear, yanking open the wardrobe. "Her things have gone."

"Maybe..."

"There's a note. There – look, on the dresser." Aoife said, quickly re-dialling the bride. "This is all very *Sleepless in Seattle* meets *Runaway Bride*. Open it – what does it say?"

Morag moved to lift the envelope from the dresser.

"And another thing – the staff have brought the breakfast into an empty fucking room. Did nobody, for a second, stop to think that actually – there should have been a woman in here who's paid a fuck-load of money to have her wedding in this poncy hotel of ours and she's not even in the fucking bridal suite?"

"I'd suggest you calmed down, but that'll be pointless when you read this," Morag said quietly.

"What does it say?" Aoife hung up the phone and threw it onto the bed.

"It says she's sorry. She's panicked and she shouldn't have let it get this far."

"Let me read it." Aoife took the letter from Morag and sat on the ottoman. Her stomach dropped.

"But the dress is still here?" Morag said with a smattering of pitiful hope.

"Ah, she's not going to take it with her now, is she?" Aoife said, hoping a more substantial letter made its way to Chris before Sarah's swift departure.

Chris, she thought. *We need to find him.*

Chapter Two

Sarah was reliably informed that it was not 'the done thing' for a bride to be so far removed from the logistics of her own wedding – several times, in fact, and mostly by her mother. It was also unbecoming of the bride to have sunburn on her wedding day. Another thing she had been told – several times, in fact, and again by her mother, who stormed around the hotel after the wedding planner with her hair swept tastefully into a chignon under tomorrow's hat while wearing yesterday's outfit, like a particularly frazzled time traveller.

She sat quietly on the terrace for most of the afternoon. Waiting, observing. The hotel staff weaved around circular tables in the shadows of the olive trees, silver cutlery glinting like miniature lighthouses in the mid-afternoon sun. Her sister, Caroline, was waltzing around tweaking chair linens and straightening placemats, all with her eldest son planted on her hip, and gesticulating to their father, Fred, who trailed behind her with arms full of eucalyptus.

Sarah was convinced that should Caro's body ever be exhumed in the name of science, they would be perplexed to find a dent in the left side of her hips caused by the arse of a child who had been wedged there since she gave birth to him. The child was less an appendage and more a particularly clingy growth.

A pale finger caressed the thin rim of her wine glass. It was why she had chosen this hotel – the wine glasses. You could tell a lot about the quality of an establishment by their glassware. Any hotel serving wine from glasses with a chunky rim and a short thick stem had found themselves quickly discounted from her shortlist, which Chris found quite a bizarre way of qualifying their future wedding venue – but who was he to argue?

Arguing was one thing they did very little of. It was the perfect-on-paper relationship. He, the sandy-haired gentle giant of a man who kept her steady and she, the forthright career woman who rarely took no for an answer.

Early in her career she had quickly learned that construction was tough industry as a woman. Sarah's success in such a male-dominated environment wasn't just about her ability to stand her ground and make her voice heard, but her eye for detail, talent for logistics and the respect she commanded from subcontractors.

She revelled in the moments when she was underestimated; mistaken for the secretary of the Project Director rather than the Project Director herself.

Yet beneath the stern exterior, she often felt the weight of constantly proving herself in a world not built for her. The long hours, the constant vigilance and the need to be twice as good to be considered half as competent. She was proud of her work, and her family were proud of her.

Sometimes her stern-work persona bled through into everyday life. Actually, it happened more often than she liked to admit. On more than one occasion as she planned her wedding, did she default into work-mode and almost made a florist cry. It was no wonder that she was so easily perceived as a raging bitch, though Chris saw through that from the beginning.

The night they met, there was no immediate spark. No cataclysmic life-changing moment that altered her outlook on life, but rather a warmth and fondness that grew with time into the most gentle and grounding of connections. On that first date, he sat opposite her nursing his red wine and watching her with thoughtful chestnut eyes. She found herself, quite unexpectedly, showing parts of herself she hadn't shown anybody since...

Well, since Sophie.

But thoughts of her were banished and had been for some time, though she couldn't ignore the flip in her stomach when even brief memories of the brunette flickered into her mind.

This was not the time to be thinking about her.

Sarah sat still, tilting her head from the shadow of the cypress trees and allowing the Mediterranean sun to warm her face. Exhaling soft plumes of silver smoke into the salty sea breeze, she closed her eyes for a moment and saw piercing blue ones staring back at her. She snapped her own eyes open, her stomach flipping once more.

She really ought to be down in the lobby with Chris, who stood like a sentry on duty diligently greeting guests as they arrived but she couldn't bring herself to it. They had the rehearsal dinner to come before the wedding, and she sat alone feigning a migraine thinking of a person who wasn't her husband-to-be.

Her life with Chris was meticulously planned, what good would it do now to allow herself to be haunted by thoughts of her former lover?

After the wedding they'd live in London for a while, but move back to Ireland after their first child. Dublin first, perhaps back to Cork eventually if they had a second. Maybe even three but they hadn't committed to that yet, but they didn't have much time. *She* didn't have much time.

They'd buy a house like Caro's, a country cottage a short walk from the coast for lazy Sunday afternoons. Retirement. Pensions. The usual rigmarole of life. She was on the cusp of her happily ever after and as it came within a hair's breadth of reality, it felt much like almost reaching the crescendo of a symphony she wasn't sure she truly liked. The notes were all there, but the melody was off somehow.

Ignoring her better judgement, she reached for her phone to scroll through her gallery for a photo she had hidden amongst thousands more.

The group of women stood beside each other, strangers to her now, grinning blindly at the camera from a nondescript bar in the middle of Farringdon they had fallen into after too many gins. There was an arm wrapped around her waist. Sarah pinched the screen and zoomed in to crop everybody else, apart from them, out of the shot. Just the two of them, frozen in time and pixels.

They had not seen each other in a two years, or was it three? Sarah didn't remember. Or she did, but would rather that she didn't. It felt like a bruise still too tender to touch, a wound that refused to heal.

What happened between them was never intentional. You could call it a flirtation which got out of hand which, in essence, was what it was.

Sarah had been with women before, on the odd occasion after a bottle of wine – cheeky smiles, friendly flirting, but she would never have even called herself curious. So, with that in mind, she could not tell you what possessed her to spend a Wednesday night alone having switched her 'Interested in' settings from men to women and swiping through West London's selection of sapphic women, but that's what happened. A moment of madness, or perhaps clarity.

She had been upfront about her intention, and she and Sophie hadn't spoken for long before agreeing to a drink the following evening after work. What began as a couple of bottles of wine in the pub, followed by an intoxicating night in darkness, was an occurrence that repeated itself more times than she should have allowed it to.

There was no question of her being gay or even bisexual. She was not and would never be, the thought hadn't even crossed her mind until... then. It didn't matter any more. She still wasn't. Sophie was an anomaly – a splendid anomaly, yes, but nevertheless a blemish or inconsistency within her dating history that was destined for doom from the start.

Then Chris came along like a comfortable pair of pyjamas after an awful day at work, and her dreams for a future were finally within arm's reach. He was what she had always wanted, that's what she told herself.

Chapter Three

S arah's phone lay face-up on the formica tabletop, its dark screen reflecting the ugly panelled lighting overhead. She was waiting for the reckoning. The shame, the panic, the consequences. The way her screen would light up like November fireworks come seven a.m.

There was no way she could go back now. Or was there?

There was nothing stopping her walking back out of the airport and taking the first taxi back to Elounda. She still had time to get ready. To grovel and apologise for her reckless impulsivity and almost walking out on the loveliest man in the world. A man who deserved better than this eleventh-hour crisis.

Chris would understand, so long as she was there in the dress she had painstakingly chosen from a dozen bridal shops, ready to commit to him. He was nothing if not forgiving, even if she didn't deserve it.

And that's when anxiety crept over her back and groped her lungs until she couldn't breathe. Is this what she actually wanted? If she wanted it, she wouldn't have run away. Or did she run away because she was scared of how much she wanted it?

After all, this was her white-picket-fence dream, wasn't it?

It was 6.55 a.m. Aoife and Morag would be coming to wake her up only to find her room empty. Chris too would be waking soon with a sore head and no idea that a broken heart would be waiting for him instead of his bride.

What the fuck was she thinking? She felt sick to her stomach.

This was not how she usually operated. How was it she could rip shreds from grown men in high-visibility jackets any day of the week, but not confide in the people who loved her the most?

Was it better, she wondered, to have continued with doubts knowing there was something not quite right, and filed for divorce if it truly was a mistake, or saved herself – and Chris – from making the mistake at all? Was she saving them both or just herself?

Well, there were few things she could do to change matters now. A coward, she was, running out on her own wedding in the middle of the night without so much as a conversation with her husband-to-be.

Behind her she had left humiliation and heartache and enough gossip to power the pensioners of Cork for at least a decade. She'd be sixty years old and still living with the whispers that had morphed from one narrative to another, ending in a bastardisation of the truth spoken by lips that were never there at all.

The shame of it would follow her around for the rest of her life.

'There she is. Over there, that's the horrible bitch who left Chris at the altar. You know, Chris O'Donnell, he used to be the sales rep for that company that sell the little blue pill our Michael keeps in the bathroom cabinet. Ah well, he probably dodged a bullet there, but he did end up marrying a lovely girl from Kerry – they've got six children now and a beautiful house by the sea. Done much better for himself.'

And then came the tirade.

It started with two calls from Aoife and Morag who took it in turns before Chris' face began to flash on screen, shortly followed by her mum and sisters Caro and Fiona – all calling one after the other. The phone fell quiet and after a few minutes, Chris' face appeared once more. Sarah stared at the screen, her finger hovering over the answer button, torn between facing the music and avoiding the inevitable for just a little longer.

She snatched the phone from the table, her mind willing her body to be brave enough to unlock and answer the phone; to whisper her apologies and plead for his forgiveness. She couldn't bear the thought of explaining to sixty guests and her childhood priest why the wedding they flew out for wasn't going ahead, but she could bear the thought of hurting Chris even less.

The hot-blooded shame crept up her neck and she shuddered.

Sarah held the phone so tightly her knuckles turned as white as the honeymoon suite. She ended the call and the voicemails mounted. How could she explain what she'd done when she had no idea why she'd done it? The only thing she did know is that marrying Chris felt disingenuous, and she was an idiot to realise it so late.

"Flight FR259 to London Stansted is now boarding at Gate Nine," the tannoy announced.

"I'm beside myself. I'm so sorry, I can't believe I've done this, and I let it get so far. I thought these doubts would go away but I couldn't go through with it and I didn't know what else to do. I promise I'll call you when I land."

Aoife read the text aloud once she had spent five minutes analysing every letter, space and apostrophe. Her responses to Sarah since had registered as undelivered so it was safe, at that point, to assume she was already mid-flight.

Sarah's mum, Finnoula, looked at her speechless with her hair in rollers and nightdress tucked hastily into her skirt. "Oh, Sarah, what have you done?" she said quietly and sat on the edge of the bed.

"At least she's safe."

"What will we do with all of the guests?" asked Finnoula, her voice tinged with panic.

"Well, Mum, I'd rather be without a wedding in Crete than in Cork," Fiona said.

"There's nothing wrong with Cork," Aoife indignantly pointed out as she leaned against the terrace table and pinched a slice of toast from the bridal breakfast selection.

"Aoife, stop eating that."

"Sarah isn't here to eat it, Morag, that's why we're stood in her room like fucking lettuces wondering how we're going to tell sixty people that the bride has done a runner."

Finnoula winced.

"Look, think back over the last couple of weeks. Can you think of anything to explain why she's gone? Has she seriously not said anything to anybody?" Caroline asked, desperately searching for clues as a toddler tugged at the hem of her pyjama top requesting to be picked up.

"Well, she disappeared mid-party last night, did you notice? I caught her legging it back to the hotel. She said she'd stained her dress..." Aoife twirled a slice of toast on the table. "...I didn't think anything of it."

"She was hardly too involved with the wedding prep yesterday, she sat up here hiding and drinking wine."

"Drinking wine is nothing new," Finnoula scoffed in Fiona's direction.

"Yes, but you know Sarah, she's eyes like a hawk – has to be in control. Don't you find it odd she wasn't doing anything?" said Morag.

"Uh, excuse me." Michael, the best man, popped his head around the door. "We're in with Chris now but Reception have told me the caterers are wanting to set up downstairs. What are we going to do with them?"

Chapter Four

Sophie's head swivelled between her laptop and her phone and back again, several times, before she placed the phone on the desk and took her head in her hands for a deep breath to stop her heart from thudding so loudly.

It didn't work. It rarely did. Her mind was racing a mile a minute as it comprehended the elation of receiving the email with the perplexity from the text that she'd received almost in the same minute.

The email came first by a fraction, and she'd devoured its contents immediately. It was the email she'd been waiting for; in fact, she'd told herself it was never going to arrive, and if it did, it would contain nothing but bad news and well-wishes. She wasn't confident enough, direct enough, good-looking enough – not that the latter should matter where employment was concerned, but somehow it always felt like it was important enough to consider when scoping the breadth of one's failings in life.

Of course, the email wouldn't never say that – they never did.

It was always 'we found a better fit for the role,' which, translated, meant *we don't like your personality, or lack thereof.* Or there was 'somebody with more experience' which really meant somebody less qualified but better at blowing their own trumpet on LinkedIn.

She knew those people. Everybody did. The ones who film themselves buying a homeless person a meal and turning it into a business pitch, or picking a crumpled crisp packet from the pavement and crafting a tenuous link between that and how good they are at selling loft insulation.

And for all their self-indulgent online presence, they were the people who always seemed to – in Sophie's eyes – get exactly what they wanted. What she wanted.

Sophie was an observer rather than a participator. Plagued by dreams of selective invisibility and the freedom to go about her business entirely unnoticed. It was difficult, though, when it came to working in Marketing – she would have been much better suited to a career in a more isolated field. Publishing, perhaps. The thought of being tucked away with novels and a notebook was a delightful one. But slowly she began to find her way – spending eight years meandering through various marketing and events roles before settling in hospitality. The behind-the-scenes world of restaurants was where she began to blossom.

How she ended up working for Hector A. Fielding, though, was anybody's guess. Actually – that was a not entirely true. He had been calm and complimentary throughout the entire hiring process, luring her into a false sense of security before revealing, approximately two months into the job – and she didn't know how he kept it to himself for that long – that he was the notoriously foul-tempered man the rest of the industry knew him to be.

'Marketing's not rocket science, any idiot can do it,' he'd say. He even went so far as to fire the Marketing Director, merge it with the Events Director role and assume Sophie would pick up the extra work with no title or salary change. Which she did without saying a word.

Boozy Lauren, the Sales Director who became her best friend, was furious with her. "You march back in there and demand what you're worth."

Sophie had shifted uncomfortably, only speaking up in protest when Lauren volunteered to do it for her.

She didn't want a fuss – of course she didn't – it was a great opportunity for her to demonstrate exactly what she was capable of.

"I don't want you getting into any trouble," Sophie said.

"My dear pal, if that cantankerous bastard was going to fire me, he'd have done it when I called him a stupid toad for standing up in the company meeting and trying to motivate us all with the phrase 'more work, fewer people,' and a shit 2003 Clipart picture of a man digging a hole," Lauren consoled, in the way only she could. "Anyway, he knows he can't fire me because I'm the only one who knows how to use Salesforce."

"You didn't call him a toad. You called him a twat."

"Yes, and he must have known he was being one or I wouldn't still be here."

"It doesn't mean you're invincible," Sophie whispered.

"No." Lauren paused. "That's true, but you just remember the moment you want to walk out I'm right behind you. That's the pact."

"That's *your* pact. You just want an excuse and a bit of drama," Sophie said. "I can't leave with nowhere to go to."

"Yes you can! People do it all the time. You've got savings. And if things get really tight, you can always sell photos of your feet to men on the internet."

She and Boozy Lauren had bonded the moment they met. The Essex-native had the confident air of a London estate agent showing you a 'one-bed self-contained flat' to rent, when in fact it was a cupboard under somebody's stairs in Walthamstow, containing nothing bar an airbed, a bucket and a bottle of bleach.

Sophie admired Lauren's semi-professional approach to recreational drinking and fully professional approach to chasing men. Lauren appreciated Sophie's commitment to finding spiritual happiness through eating enough pasta to feed the armies of Eastern Europe and her never-ending tolerance of their bulbous prick of a boss.

The pair were united in their mutual dislike of Hector. A portly man in his fifties, a former restaurant critic, notoriously short of temper to the point where he was fired by *The Independent* for launching a tray of sandwiches across a meeting room at the Managing Editor when he heard the size of his column was being halved. Sometimes Sophie wished she'd heard that story *before* accepting the job.

This email though was an end to all of that.

It was validating in the best sort of way – the sort with nobody looking at her. She'd actually stood up to scrutiny and this email was proof that somebody saw in her what she knew was there.

The sender, Gennaro, was a different breed of man to Hector. The latter was a man of five foot seven, plump of stature and pompous of nature. Demanding, abrasive and generally ignorant of how the world, and his own business, truly worked, he was completely reliant on those around him to do the thinking for him and was the first to throw the book when he interfered and caused things to go pear-shaped.

Whereas silver-haired Gennaro stood taller. He was a quiet, thoughtful man, who seemed to genuinely value the contribution his team made to his business. He waited for somebody to finish speaking before taking his turn and took the time to consider his options rather than make rash decisions that affected not only him but his team.

To Gennaro, his team were crucial to the success of his business. To Hector, his business would be successful if he had a team or not.

She might be a lesbian, but she could appreciate Gennaro's appeal to women of a more heterosexual persuasion and had already made a mental note that she would keep Boozy Lauren from crossing his path.

Though she had to admit, Lauren had a way with men that she found fascinating, and men always found it thrilling to meet a woman who was confident enough to chat them up, instead of the other way around.

Lauren had actually met her last boyfriend at a bus stop in Balham. She looked at his hand as he fished his debit card from his pocket and said, 'Did you know, if your index finger is shorter than your fourth finger on your right hand, then statistically you're more likely to be a criminal?' and the rest was history.

Or it was for about four months until she found out he painted Warhammer figurines and that was enough for her to 'bin him off' and divert her attentions to a Polish waiter they'd met at Café Rouge in Hampstead.

Gennaro's offer was generous. Irresistible, even. It was an opportunity for a complete life overhaul, and God knows she felt like she was in need of one. She had been living in London for twelve years and felt that little had changed in that time, other than she'd started growing hair in places she hadn't had hair before.

She saw her friends back home in Manchester settling down, buying houses, having children – or, if not that, at least living alone in their own spaces. No bumping into strangers in their own living room because their housemate had brought somebody home and they'd been shagging on the sofa all night. No turning up to housemate interviews like an awkward spotty teenager hoping to be invited to dance and praying they like you enough to offer you their box room in Queen's Park for nine hundred pounds a month.

London, for all its wonder and opportunity, propelled you forward in some ways and held you back in others. She was twenty-nine and still living with a housemate (at least it wasn't three, she told herself), still trying to stash money into savings and have some semblance of a social life in an increasingly expensive city, while working for a boss who wouldn't even entertain the idea of a pay rise.

What she would love, more than anything, at this point in her life was to have a place where she could leave crumbs on the counter and pots in the sink. To have long baths on a Saturday night without somebody wanting to use the toilet. To be able to go to the bathroom in the middle of the night without bumping into Craig sleepwalking with his testicles out.

And she could have all of that, by just responding to Gennaro's email. Right there and then, saying 'yes, I will take the job.'

Her hands hovered over the keyboard. Her heart continued hammering and her temperature rose until she was sure she was flushed in the face.

What's the reality here? she thought. *You can't just jump headfirst into the unknown.* She didn't have to respond right away; Gennaro's offer was seemingly without an immediate deadline, and she could move at her own pace. The job was hers and he was 'in no rush'.

She'd need to check her notice period with HR and hope word didn't get back to Hector. He'd take sadistic pleasure in making her working life even more intolerable than it already was. She'd need to put her furniture into storage, and find a new flatmate for Craig – but not before she'd told her friends and family that she was about to make one hell of a life change.

She could already imagine the anxiety-filled texts from her mother, forewarning her against various absurd and hypothetical dangerous situations inspired by something she'd seen on a Monday night crime drama.

'If somebody hands you a scratchcard in the street, don't stand there and scratch it. It's a human trafficking trap – they want you to stay still so they can grab you and put you in a van.' or 'I've heard the factory that make Polos have been secretly lacing them with GHB'.

Sophie could only imagine what she'd say about her moving to Italy. 'Don't join the Mafia, will you?' or, 'Please don't start selling drugs if money gets tight, we'll always help you.' As if either were realistic possibilities.

Then again, she imagined women in the Mafia to be quite attractive. And as she felt herself drifting off into dreams of *la dolce vita,* her phone buzzed on her desk and thoughts of wine, pasta and Italian women were cut short by a text from an unknown number.

She hadn't noticed how the clatter of fingers slamming against keyboards had died down and she was one of only a handful of people left in the office. Tourists on Regent Street periodically pressed their hands and faces to the semi-opaque glass to see what lay behind. Shadows crept up sandy-brick walls and white linen curtains brushed softly against each other in the breeze of the air conditioning.

17:02: Unknown number – I know it's been a while, but I've done something stupid. Can we meet for a drink tonight? Sarah x

Chapter Five

Sophie's heart stopped for a second, then returned to thudding in her ears. Her throat went dry. The internet therapy videos she had watched online over the past two years replayed in her head all at once.

Delete the message and move on.

Send a polite thank you but no thank you *and wish her the best.*

She was over it. Water under the bridge. She didn't need to meet Sarah for a drink. What would she gain?

But then again, if she were over it, then it wouldn't really matter. She had moved on. She had a new life in Italy on the horizon and it wasn't like they had parted on bad terms. They could meet as friends, for a drink, a catch-up. Two women who knew they never had a forever and who wanted the best for each other.

It would all be very civil. Very grown up. Very European actually, she thought.

And though there was nothing to gain from meeting for a drink, she was also propelled by an intense nosiness that had followed her from childhood.

What on earth could be so bad that she'd turned to Sophie after years of no-contact?

Curiosity was certainly the reason why they'd become involved in the first place. It was an experiment, a chance for Sophie to prove that she could indeed have no-strings sex.

It was not an experiment with the outcome she'd hoped for.

It got out of hand. The variables were not monitored nor boundaries ever discussed and so feelings became involved. They'd accidentally ended up in a quasi-relationship without ever really realising and so by circumstance, it was doomed to fail from the start.

Not to mention that Sarah was vehemently straight, despite prior actions indicating otherwise.

So while Sophie really wanted to pretend she hadn't read text and return to planning her new life, she couldn't not find out what was behind such an uncharacteristic message from her ex.

She rested the corner of her phone on her bottom lip as she contemplated her response. The answer was of course going to be yes, or the unknown would bite away at her all week.

They might have been a mistake but they were besotted. Back then, at least.

Before meeting Sarah, Sophie had three golden rules when it came to dating. The first was to ensure they texted for at least four days to filter out the emotionally unstable, the women who had boyfriends and those who had the personality of a potato. She couldn't be the only one to carry a conversation, or they'd never speak at all.

The second rule was no sex on the first date. Not necessarily because she was a prude, or formed an emotional attachment the moment she had sex – this was more about logistics.

First dates had to be a weeknight. Why waste a weekend night on somebody you'd never met? It was too much of a gamble. So if you're on a date on a weeknight and you go back to somebody's house completely spontaneously, you're faced with the dilemma of either having to call in sick to work to mask the fact you slept in a foreign bed and drank far too many margaritas – or turn up to work in yesterday's clothes with a violent hangover. Or worse still – turning up to a first date with a spare set of clothes and have them run a mile from you for appearing too presumptuous. The latter was never, ever an option. Ever.

Hangovers are anxiety-inducing enough as they are, Sophie thought. The last thing she needed was for everybody to know she had one and that she'd been up to no good to get it. That was anxiety layered on anxiety, like an emotionally turbulent lasagne.

The third rule, and in her opinion the most important, was to date experienced sapphics because it was no good becoming emotionally entangled with somebody still trying to figure themselves out. It was a one way ticket to heartbreak.

While the logic behind these rules were sound, if you were to ask Sophie why she threw them all out of the window for a date with Sarah, she wouldn't have been able to give you the same answer twice.

17:11: Sophie – Sure. I can be free at 8. The Chamberlayne?

As if Lauren had been summoned by the thought of a wine bottle cracking open, she slid up to Sophie's desk.

"Are you going to come for a drink? You look like you need one."

"Is that code for saying that I look like shit?"

"Yes. You're looking all... clammy."

"I am?" Sophie said, worried. She'd have to make sure she showered before seeing Sarah. She didn't want to look desperate and dishevelled. She wanted to turn up looking like she'd seen nothing but success in the years since they said a teary goodbye in Ladbroke Grove.

She felt strange. Was it really such a good idea to meet Sarah when there was so much left unsaid between them?

"Come on," said Lauren, interrupting her internal spiralling, "something is wrong and I want to know what's up. Come for a drink with me."

"I, erm, I can't. I'm meeting Sarah."

"Sorry, what now?" Lauren paused. "Did I hear 'Sarah'? As in *the* Sarah. The Sarah you told me all about when I started here and who you should have never got involved with?"

"Yep, that's the one," said Sophie.

"No you're not."

"Yes I am. Something's happened and–"

"And nothing, it's not your responsibility."

Sophie was almost thrilled to see Hector storming out of the boardroom in his pinstripe suit with his hallmark forehead vein bulging and retracting. While he was the same height as Sophie, Lauren took great delight in peering down at his poorly-covered bald patch from her five-foot-ten point of view.

"Have you seen these figures?" he demanded, waving a pile of papers in Sophie's direction.

"They're still in your hand," Lauren smirked. Hector looked up, previously oblivious to her presence.

"Here." He thrust the papers towards Sophie.

"How, erm, how urgent is this, Hector?" she asked apprehensively. "It's just – I've, erm, I've got to go. I tell you what, though – I'll read them on the train, yeah? And I'll come back to you tomorrow."

Hector looked flummoxed and Lauren felt a sense of pride in Sophie for not jumping to his demands immediately. Admittedly it wasn't how she'd have handled it, she'd have told him to get stuffed, but it was certainly a start.

He said nothing and squinted suspiciously at Lauren and Sophie in turn. Sophie stood to unplug her laptop and pack her bag. She made sure to place the papers carefully in her bag and grimaced at Hector until he strode away to bark demands at his assistant, Ana.

Boozy Lauren grabbed her jacket and bag to follow Sophie out of the door.

"So is that why you're in some weird daze, because Sarah's text you?"

Sophie paused on the corner of Hanover Square and reached for the emergency cigarette she pretended she didn't keep in her coat pocket.

"Sophie?" Lauren prompted, pinching the lit cigarette and taking a drag.

"Look, it's just a quick drink. A catch-up – there'll be no knicker-ripping and hopping into bed together. It's been two years, it'll be fine. And I also want to find out what was so bad that she's asked to meet me."

"Okay, so I kind of want to know too, but not enough for you to go gallivanting off and getting your heart broken again."

Sophie paused and watched Lauren inhale what had been her last cigarette. She was reluctant to buy any more because it meant she'd become a *smoker*.

"You've had more of that cig than I have."

"I did it for your health." said Lauren. "Look, there's clearly nothing I can say that will change your mind. Once you've got your sights set on something... you'll do it anyway. Just... please be careful, keep your knickers on and tell me everything when you're home."

The late summer sun wrapped Kensal Rise in a lazy orange glow, soon to be eclipsed by tall terraces casting their grand shadows over the last of the stragglers sitting outside into the evening. On a quiet street off Chamberlayne Road, where the roots of trees jolted the flagstones out of place and leaves rustled contentedly in a soft wind, was a pub rendered white and known only to locals.

Sophie had raced home, speeding past the tourists dawdling down Regent Street and scattering them like skittles. She caught the Overground at Euston, by all means the quickest way to be home within fifteen minutes so she had the time to look put-together, but not in a polished *I-tried-to-make-an-effort-for-you* sense, in a more nonchalant *I-always-look-like-this* approach.

That nonchalant approach took an hour to perfect, and even then she had fiddled with her fringe constantly as she walked to the pub to make sure it sat just right.

Anticipation had grown in her belly from the moment she left the office. Curiosity killed the cat, as they say, but what harm could this meet really do?

For a second, Sophie leant against the dark polished doorframe and watched Sarah, noticing how her caramel curls were scraped back into a clip as she stared listlessly at the coffee in front of her.

Sarah looked up at her with pink-rimmed eyes and grimaced. "Hi. Sorry, I look a state."

"Do you want me to get you something? White? Rosé?" Sarah made the move to go to the bar.

"No, no. Thank you." Sophie sat still, observing the woman sitting opposite. The soft waves of her hair lightened with subtle blonde highlights framed delicate features, the pale skin Sophie remembered kissed slightly by the sun.

They sat soaking in the other's presence until Sarah broke the silence.

"Thank you... for coming to meet me. I know it seems a little out of the blue... I just didn't know who else to – I've been asleep and hiding in bed all day..." Sarah's voice broke and she sniffed.

"So..." Sophie prompted.

Sarah opened her mouth to speak and hesitated; she gulped, gathering herself for a moment. "I was... getting married. Crete. I was getting married in Crete and I, uh, I left," she whispered. "Chris... he was, I mean *is* lovely. Wonderful, even. Any woman would be lucky to have him... but not me. I mean, I was lucky to have him but... marrying him. It wouldn't have been right. I'd have been robbing him, really, of who he was supposed to be with. Somebody who... loved him as much as he loved her..."

There – she'd said it out loud without realising in a stream-of-consciousness thought. Her lips stopped in their tracks as she processed what had left them. He was almost too perfect but if she couldn't be happy with him, truly and carefreely happy, then what was wrong with her?

"So you just left?" Sophie asked incredulously, settling back into her seat.

"I panicked, I suppose. Who organises an entire wedding... flies a priest out to fucking Crete and the whole hog, just to back out at the last minute? The shame of it... explaining to all those people you've made a massive mistake," said Sarah. "Chris... the poor creature. I've been awful. A rancid bitch for doing it but... I couldn't. I couldn't see the pain I'd caused him... so I ran. Middle of the night, just... went."

Sophie sighed at the dishevelled woman sitting before her.

"I wanted it... I did or I wouldn't have - gone so far as I did," Sarah continued. "But then it just dawned on me, you know, the finality of it all. I was scared... something wasn't sitting right. He was, *is*, a genuinely faultless man which makes what I've done even worse. There's something wrong with me... there's got to be. Why couldn't I be as excited to marry him as he was to marry me?"

"I think it's too late for me, you know, Sophie. I'm thirty-nine and what do I have to show for it? The one chance I had, gone. I ruined it."

Sarah clawed at her lips. "Please don't hate me for bringing you here. I knew you'd listen without jumping down my throat. I had to talk to somebody. I had to talk to *you*."

Chapter Six

Sarah awoke on the sofa, her eyes crusted shut with sleep and her left arm numb. She rubbed her face and dabbed at the saliva leaking ungracefully from the corner of her mouth. For a few seconds, her sleepy haze lingered and she found a moment of ignorant bliss before a persistent buzzing started to emanate from the coffee table.

Clumsy hands scrambled and jabbed the screen.

"Hi Mam?" Her voice croaked down the phone, still thick with fatigue.

"Oh thank God, Sarah, are you OK? Where are you? It's OK, I've got her, I've got her." She could be heard shouting to somebody in the background.

"I'm just... I'm just home."

"Home in Ireland or home in London?"

"London, Mam."

"Right, OK. Are you all right? What happened? Tell me everything. Why didn't you come and speak to one of us?"

Sarah's entire body ached as she sat upright and tucked her knees underneath her chin.

"Oh Mam," she began to weep, "I've really fucked up, haven't I?"

"I wish you'd have spoken to someone, Sarah. I just want to understand. Chris needs to understand."

"What will people say?"

"That doesn't matter. Just talk to me, love."

"I just, I just got so – so scared. I couldn't marry him, Mam, it wouldn't have been fair to do it while I was having so many doubts about whether it was what I really wanted. I mean, I do love him, he's such a kind man and didn't deserve this at all, but it wouldn't have been fair to go through with it and divorce three months later…" her words tumbled out of her mouth like rocks crashing down a cliff face, each quicker than the last and landing without consequence. "I shouldn't have let it go that far, I thought I'd buried everything and then it came flooding back and I couldn't do it."

Sarah stared intently at the fireplace in front of her. When they moved in, she became obsessed with making the flat absolutely picture perfect for their life together. Every corner and crevice was filled, plastered, painted and polished to within an inch of its life, yet it was the fireplace that she saw as the Victorian copper cherry on the cake.

In fact, the entire flat, Chris' flat, was the result of her time and effort, which would have been worth it had she done what she had promised and married the man. But instead she was sitting on the sofa with wet cheeks, seriously considering the pros and cons of opening a bottle of wine at eleven a.m.

"We're sorting everything here, everybody has been incredibly understanding and you don't need to worry about anything. What will you do for a place to stay?"

She looked around hopelessly; she couldn't stay there. Everything was a memento of their time together; the vase they bought in Notting Hill from a man she was sure was out to con them, but Chris knew she wanted it so bought it anyway for far more than it was probably worth. The colour of the bedroom, periwinkle; they'd had a blazing row over whether Chris had bought the right colour because it looked more grey.

Even the kitchen tongs which he would not throw out, even though they were pretty much broken, just because his mother had bought them and he wouldn't want her to be upset.

"What, uh, what about Chris? Have you spoken to him?"

"I've been to give him a hug but he's not one for talking at the moment. He just needs a little time..."

"Yes... yes, you're right..."

"Your father and I are going to come to London..."

"No!" Sarah interjected. "I mean, please, you don't need to. I think I just need my own company at the moment to figure things out."

"Are you sure?"

"Yes, yes, thank you."

"Okay, I need to run off and check on the kids because Charlie's running rings around Caroline and baby Conan is screaming his little head off. Sarah, ring me if you need anything. Please try and get some rest, things will seem much better when you have."

Sarah flopped back onto the couch with a dull thud and stared dry-eyed at the ceiling.

The door buzzed.

"Hello? Is that Mrs O'Donnell?"

That felt like a punch to the stomach.

"Who – who is this?"

"This is your delivery driver, I've a case of champagne here for you."

"Can you... can you... can you leave it there please? I'll send... I'll fetch it... later. Later. Yes, thank you."

Mrs O'Donnell. She didn't know when Chris would be back home and though it wouldn't be soon, she still couldn't spend another moment there knowing the history it had and the future it didn't. But where would she go?

A hotel, perhaps. In the short term it would do but in the long term she would need somewhere else to live. She might be spontaneously single and through her own doing, but she still needed to work. There was no way she was going to move back to her Mam and Dad's. No, that was one step too far.

I cannot believe I'm thirty-fucking-nine and have to move into a flat share, she thought.

Chapter Seven

"Are you ready yet? We need to leave in fifteen minutes," shouted a voice from the kitchen that grew closer before its owner crashed through the door with two drinks.

"I hope you didn't spill any on the carpet, I only cleaned yesterday..." Sophie muttered.

"Shut up and drink up."

"Remind me who we're meeting again?"

"His name is Mark, he's a financial advisor based in Old Street but he lives in South Kensington. He has salt and pepper hair, real daddy vibes–" Craig began, handing her a vodka and tonic.

"I'm just going to stop you there. It's not him I'm interested in. Who's the friend I'm entertaining and why is she even coming? Can't it just be the two of you?"

Craig sighed. "She's visiting him from Sussex, staying at his flat. He feels bad leaving her so I thought I'd bring my favourite lesbian to meet his favourite lesbian. See? Match made in heaven, he and I."

"But what does she look like? What's her name? Is she femme, masc, androgynous? You know how I get when I have to pretend to be interested in somebody, so give me something to go on here."

"I think she's a plumber called Steph..." Craig began, but stopped when he saw the look on Sophie's face. "I'm *joking*, I think she's called

Katie and she's got some fancy job – an architect, no, a designer. Something like that."

Making small talk with a stranger just so her housemate could get his leg over was far from her ideal Friday night, especially when she had been so looking forward to having the flat to herself. She had a feeling that her plans of drinking wine in the bath were about to be scuppered when Craig came home earlier that evening with a bottle of cava and a card for 'the best friend ever'.

'He's attractive so I'm sure his friends are hot too,' Craig had bargained, 'and anyway, you haven't been on a date in a million years. I bet you have cobwebs in your knickers. Oh go on, Sophie, please.'

They met in a bar in Berkeley Square where chic women and dapper men swanned across marble floors. Copper statues of naked women were suspended in the air above the tan leather banquettes that lined the room, its walls built of backlit agate.

Craig made a beeline for a sharply dressed man with grey temples fading into jet-black hair, a tasteful tan and chiselled chin. By his side was a woman – Katie, it was safe to bet – who was as tall as Sophie with long platinum hair. She was attractive, she'd give Craig that, but what she soon found out was that she had the personality of a taxidermied ferret.

Mark and Craig were getting along famously. She nodded and smiled as Katie talked about fashion week and sourcing buttons from the arse-end of China or something to that effect, because the real conversation she was interested in was the one being had at the table beside them.

He had Mediterranean heritage, did Mark. Italian, actually, on his mother's side. A wave of excitement shuddered down her spine.

Craig would be devastated at the thought of having to find a stranger to live with in her place. Or she hoped he would be after four years of living together. Perhaps she could persuade Boozy Lauren to move in.

After all, they got on like a house on fire and, though she wasn't gay, she certainly had been mistaken for a lesbian frequently when they went out in Soho.

'It's the Superdry coat,' Sophie told her. 'My Auntie gave me this,' Lauren protested. 'I understand that,' Sophie responded, 'but it's a lesbian calling card and that's why you get all the attention and I look like your sympathetic straight friend.'

Katie had stopped with her spiel mid-sentence to scroll through the emails on her phone.

Sophie also felt her phone buzzing. "Sorry, I've got to take this. It's work, you know how it is…" she lied and left the table to answer. The other woman didn't even lift her head and Craig was too lost in Mark's eyes to notice.

"Hey, are you awake?" said an Irish lilt at the other end.

Shit. In her eagerness to find a distraction, she hadn't even looked at who was calling. She hadn't heard from Sarah in almost two weeks.

"Yeah, you'll have to speak up though."

"Oh, sorry, if you're out then I'll…"

"Don't worry. What's up?"

Sophie could hear Sarah pause and take a deep breath at the other end of the line. Sophie's stomach tensed in anticipation.

"Do you want to come over for a glass of wine?"

She could hear Lauren and Craig's voices in the back of her mind saying, *Sophie, don't you fucking dare,* and then she felt her breath catch in her throat.

"Only if it's good wine," Sophie said, ignoring her better judgement.

"Of course it is. How long will you be?"

Sophie was usually the first to admit when she'd done something stupid. And it happened more often than she would care to acknowledge. Like with most acts of stupidity, she knew what she was doing while she was doing it, but not once did it stop her in her tracks and force her to reconsider. So it was no surprise to anybody, least of all herself, that she had fucked up again.

It wasn't as if she'd legged it around London with glittery nipples and stood in the middle of Finsbury Park to declare herself a one-woman nation, but landing in bed with her ex-girlfriend was hardly her smartest idea. She should have seen it coming.

The hangover was a Code Red alarm, she had decided before even opening her eyes. The worst kind – thoroughly debilitating, rendering her useless even for holding a conversation and most likely to result in a tactical vomit on a Tube station platform.

She felt the familiar rumination of nausea creeping from her belly and acid burning in her throat. A headache, caused by a concoction of wine and lack of sleep, drove her to bury her head under the duvet and away from the white-hot pins of light poking in through the shutter blinds.

Drunk Sophie, in her infinite wisdom, had left a pint of water by the bed which she downed in haste. Instant regret. It threatened to make a reappearance already.

Her pillow buzzed. Whether it was her phone or a vibrator was anybody's guess.

Boozy Lauren was calling. This time on a Saturday? A hate crime.

09:08: Sophie – Text later.

Sophie gulped to keep down the watery vomit threatening to drag her into the bathroom and from the warmth of the bed. She groaned, then somebody else did too. A beeping followed, a persistent noise permeating the silence that slept between them.

Who the fuck is that? And what is that beeping? She hadn't opened her eyes fully, but when she did she realised this was not her bed.

She had never been in this room before. There was a pale mass of blonde-cum-brown curls on the pillow beside hers, and their owner was most definitely naked. *Oh, for God's sake, Sophie.*

She bolted from the bed to the bathroom and vomited into the sink; thankfully Sarah hadn't stirred.

There was red lipstick smudged up her cheek and mascara crescents under her eyes. Her fringe, usually poker-straight, stuck up at all angles. She scraped her chestnut hair into a ponytail so she didn't vomit in it.

Attractive, yes, that's me, Sophie thought. *All my hard work has come undone. Therapy Jeff would be so disappointed in me – if he knew I existed.*

She cast her mind back to the night before and even the thought of drinking was enough to initiate a projectile vomit, retching as quietly as she could into the toilet. She cursed the bad date with Katie, she cursed herself for ever answering the phone and she cursed her complete lack of willpower for Sarah and for wine too.

This was an absolutely terrible idea by all accounts.

Sophie splashed her face and returned to bed, propped herself up on the pillows and imagined this was what life might be like if she were a bedridden pensioner in a Victorian drama.

Lost in her thoughts, she flirted with the idea of giving up alcohol entirely. She could be like her aunt, who always said *less wine, more Louboutins.* Sophie could go dry and break up with alcohol. But then, she thought, what if, in doing so, she shrivelled up like a raisin? She was too young to look like a camel's testicle.

Anyway, what if she became the type of person who turned down a chilled glass of Sancerre 'to keep a clear head,' or heaven forbid, she became a person who *ran?* She would surely give her father a heart attack if she voluntarily took up exercise. Lauren would raise her eyebrows so high they'd fuse to her hairline and Craig would disown her entirely. No, she decided, she had better keep drinking for the good of her health, her father's and her friends. It was safer for everybody.

She dry-heaved again. *I've got to stop thinking about alcohol,* she thought, and dragged herself out of bed to open the blinds slightly.

Golden light danced on the waxy leaves of the bushes that shaded the window and kept her modesty hidden from the odd passing pedestrian. Dozens of Edwardian terraced houses sat politely side by side. Women in head-to-toe Lycra and thick-soled trainers bounced down the street with buggies in front of them making a mockery of Sophie's current state of despair.

Fresh air would do her good. The chill in the morning air would slap her senses back into her and she'd forget about the night before and the feelings it aroused. The memories of hot lips and hotter skin, teeth biting, limbs knotted together and heads thrown back with lips cast open in silent *oh*s, before two writhing bodies fell still in the dead of night, reunited and gasping for breath.

Chapter Eight

They took to sitting on the oak floor, nursing a glass of wine apiece, underneath the bay window which Sarah had cracked open slightly to allow the cigarette smoke a place of escape.

The yellow glow of the streetlamps crept through the overgrown shrubbery and cast a soft light on Sarah's face, highlighting the soft lines around the corners of her eyes and apples of her cheeks.

"I don't know what I'm doing, Sophie." Sarah turned and looked at her sheepishly. Every move she made and word she uttered was considered and measured, yet she was still lost.

"Nobody does. We're all fumbling around with the light switched off, you know." Sophie sipped her wine.

"I'm sorry. I don't know why I asked you here. I don't know why you agreed to come. I know I hurt you."

Sophie remembered pausing for a while before responding.

"You did..." she replied softly, her voice just a whisper. She repetitively ran her finger around the rim of the glass to avoid looking up. "Do you want me to leave?"

"What? No, of course not. Unless you want to?" Sarah added tentatively.

"No. I'm quite happy here drinking your wine."

"Where were you tonight?"

"Craig roped me into a double date with some man he's into and his friend."

"Oh."

"Don't 'Oh' me, like I haven't moved on, especially when you almost got married!" Sophie laughed.

"Piss off, you daft bollocks." Sarah smiled and pushed Sophie's leg playfully. She tucked her ankles underneath her and leant forward towards Sophie. Her eyes had darkened as she dropped her gaze to Sophie's collarbone and down her body.

A hesitant finger reached for Sophie's outstretched ankle and started to draw light patterns on soft, bare skin, leaving the light tingle of her touch on the top of her foot and up the back of her calf. Two pairs of eyes followed the daring dance of swoops and swirls up to the hem of Sophie's skirt and back behind her knee in agonisingly slow rotations.

The drawing stopped. Sophie watched Sarah, who had moved closer still, her parted lips emitting shallow, silent breaths. If time could have moved slower then it would surely have stopped entirely. Sarah raised her hand again and cupped the face she had studied with such intensity. A warm thumb brushed Sophie's cheek, bringing her palm to rest before pushing her fingers back to weave them through deep brown hair.

"Can I kiss you?"

And that was the story, from what she remembered anyway. The reason behind her stinking headache, persistent nausea and finding herself naked next to her recently single ex-girlfriend.

Sophie sighed.

10:45: Lauren – Meet me for brunch in North Weezy?

11:03: Sophie – I've never heard that abbreviation before I and I hope I never will again. Where do you want to go?

11:05: Lauren – North West. I'm in Queen's Park. Come on, I'll buy you a drink. I want to hear about your date.

Sophie's stomach lurched. Brunch with Lauren only ever led to one thing – a string of bad decisions. But what was another bad decision or two on top of the one she made last night? She and Sarah would have to talk about it but having that conversation on a hangover was too much.

"I've got to go and meet Lauren," Sophie said to the nest of curls hiding the face pushed against the pillow.

"Tell her you're sick today, stay here with me," Sarah purred, her voice thick with sleep as she absent-mindedly trailed a finger down Sophie's bare back, a small comfort in her sorry state.

She supposed that if she stayed, she wouldn't need to tell Lauren the truth, nor lie to her, but at some point she would need to choose one or the other. She would go ballistic.

If she left now she could make it. Why was Wandsworth such a pain to travel from? Why did she even agree to go there? There were so many questions, and Lauren would launch into a thousand more; she was a one-woman Spanish Inquisition.

There was no way it was sensible to stay there, in that bed, that lovely warm bed, with Sarah.

Naked Sarah.

Perhaps her rampant hangover would implore her to be sensible. Surely it couldn't end too badly if she kept her wits about her, and it certainly wouldn't end like the last brunch did; in a Soho strip club called Forbidden Nights with Lauren licking cream from a stripper's nipple. She turned on her back and Sarah came to sleep on her chest as if no time had passed.

God, she needed a bacon sandwich.

After a pep talk and twenty minutes of mustering the courage to move, Sophie sat up again and a door elsewhere in the flat slammed shut. Sarah yanked her back into the sheets.

"Wha–"

"Shhh," she hissed. "It's Helen, my housemate."

"Sorry, what housemate?"

Sarah pressed her index finger to her lips and hissed, "You can't go yet. You'll have to wait until she's gone to the gym."

Bollocks. Sophie listened intently as this mystery figure waltzed in a leisurely manner about the house, turning the shower on and off again, slamming the bathroom cabinet, until the train of noises finished with the front door decidedly locking.

They waited with bated breath until there was no sign of Helen returning. Sophie looked about the room to locate her clothes, strewn in an impressive variety of distances and directions, before dressing hastily and stumbling through the front door into the bright light of morning, with her throbbing feet forced into last night's heels, and setting her destination to Clapham Junction.

What she had not bargained for was for her legs to feel unsteady, and for the thought of boarding the Tube with a hundred sweaty bodies pushed against her to cause her to vomit on the pavement in front of two horrified children. "That lady is just feeling poorly," she heard their adult say, swiftly crossing the road with them while she paused to sit on the closest garden wall.

12:09: Sophie – I need to stop home first. I am not a well woman.

She would get a taxi. It would save her having to get off the train at regular intervals and pretend to the station guards that she had morning sickness. She was not proud of the excuse but it certainly was effective in ensuring they stayed at least four feet away from the nauseous-looking woman staring listlessly into space.

There was no place in Heaven for her, she decided, thinking back to the time her Dad placed a Bible on her forehead to see if she started smoking.

Though she contemplated skipping brunch entirely. She *should* have skipped brunch entirely, gone straight home to bed and not left it until eleven p.m, but instead she called a cab.

Lauren was sitting in the Alice House. Its stripped bare bricks and industrial lighting reminded her of their office.

The early September sun bounced off the windscreens of cars she had no chance of affording in this life. She was sitting in the middle of the room, surrounded by weekend luvvies swapping tales of their weeks over poached eggs and avocado with a glass of fizz apiece. True to form, Lauren was herself nursing a glass of prosecco with another one poured and ready for Sophie.

Sophie tried everything in her power not to baulk at the smell of food and sight of alcohol. She failed miserably and bolted towards the toilets. Lauren had underestimated the intensity of her friend's hangover, and on seeing her, reached out and claimed the second glass for herself, knowing it wouldn't be touched otherwise.

"What on earth happened to you? I want to know everything."

"My soul has left my body. If I die, make sure I'm buried in red lipstick," Sophie groaned.

"Are those the clothes you went out in last night?"

"Do I look that rough?"

"You do look fairly atrocious." Lauren laughed. "It was a success, then?"

"It was certainly eventful. We just got drunk and that led to... well, this."

"What's she like then, Katie?"

"She's..."

Boring? Self-absorbed? Perfect for somebody who doesn't like the sound of their own voice? Ideal for somebody who cannot speak for themselves? All of the above, perhaps. Not the woman for Sophie, but she wasn't ready to tell Lauren that.

Lauren's eyes widened expectantly, impatiently waiting for the details to emerge of her raucous night with a new woman. Then again, there was no reason why she couldn't substitute one name for another. *A genius idea,* she thought, knowing Lauren would be too wrapped up in the debauchery to question any minor inconsistencies.

"Interesting. Well, I also pulled last night," Lauren announced when the story had finished and asked for a top-up from the waiter. "And another green tea, for my sorry friend over here."

"Which poor man have you harangued this time? Was it the one with a face like a barnacle you met at The Stag?"

"Oh no, not him. He had as much of a sense of humour as a brick to the face. Which reminds me, we've got to add The Stag to the list of pubs we can't go back to. Anyway, he's called Marcus, or Michael, anyway, it's a funny story actually. I was waiting at the cash machine outside the Paradise near your flat and I got talking to the bloke in front of me. Anyway, the next thing I know, I'm giving him a handjob in the Uber back to his house and we spent all night shagging."

The last sentence she proclaimed so loudly that the four blonde girls on the adjacent table looked over and started to whisper amongst themselves.

"Anyway," Lauren dropped her voice to a whisper, "I'm not sure whether all the sex sobered me up or made me worse."

"I don't think I tell you often enough what an over-sharer you are." Sophie laughed.

"And then we just kept waking each other up in the middle of night and–"

Sophie held her hands up. "I don't think I need any more details, thank you."

Lauren began to demolish her breakfast with the fervour of a famished gorilla. Sophie took the break in the inquisition to check her phone. One unread message from Sarah. She felt a flicker of excitement in her stomach and quickly admonished herself for it.

The fragmented recollections of her night still left her hot under the collar, even though it ought not to have happened.

Sarah had broken up with her fiancé and left him at the altar Crete only a few days before – an absurdity in itself, before adding their rekindled situationship into the mix.

14:54: Sarah – We should probably talk. Will you come back tonight? x

Was she having regrets? Did she want to pick up where they left off? No, that was a stupid question – Sophie did not want Sarah. It went pear-shaped last time and it would do so again if they pursued it.

She paused.

Oh, the panic was rising and she had to keep her cool or Lauren would be suspicious. She had already launched into a line of questioning about

'Katie' that only stopped short of asking what her National Insurance number was.

14:57: Sophie – Sure, will be about 7. Meet you halfway in Shepherd's Bush?

"You all right, mate?" Lauren piped up between mouthfuls of waffles.

"Erm, yeah. Katie wants to see me again tonight." Sophie lied.

Chapter Nine

Autumn clouds already started to clip at the heels of the sun. Sophie drew her grey suede jacket tighter around her shoulders and pushed her head down through the wind gathering force down Burrows Road towards the Overground.

The sudden change in weather came as a shock to the system after an almost unbearably warm summer. Sophie mourned the many sunny evenings spent drinking wine on the banks of Little Venice with Lauren, fantasising what they would do with Hector's company if he were to disappear in not-so-suspicious circumstances.

Lauren would immediately shut down Hector's vanity project restaurants, instead opting for more sensible sites in up-and-coming locations with a higher return on investment. 'Nobody needs another dickhead restaurant in Knightsbridge, Soph,' she'd said. She'd fire the current contractors and hire a team of buff builders that only worked shirtless. 'Like Butlers in the Buff, but Builders in the Buff.'

The first thing Sophie would do would be to hire a more ruthless HR department to protect the company from any improper conduct grievances caused by Lauren hiring naked builders. She'd expand overseas into Europe, opening a line of small hotels and running wellness getaways, and use that as her opportunity to leave London.

Her dream for Hector's company was the job she had been offered by Gennaro already – as the Head of Marketing for his small chain of family-run hotels dotted about Tuscany. It was at this point she had almost slipped up until Lauren chimed in with 'But no, you can't leave me here. What will I do without you?' and she choose to keep her mouth shut.

It felt too good to be true – and this was the only thing stopping her from jumping into the opportunity with both feet. She had thanked Gennaro that afternoon for his offer and trust in her, asking him for time to consider the logistics of relocating before confirming her acceptance.

He responded quickly and kindly. They could manage while she got her affairs in order.

Her first meeting with the hotelier was a chance encounter. She had spent the evening of Hector's latest restaurant opening, Koyote in Mayfair, darting from journalist to content creator to photographer and door host, too busy to notice eyes watching her like a hawk.

He wasn't on the invite list. Gennaro was a plus-one who had spontaneously accepted the invite from a food critic friend only an hour prior to doors opening.

Only once appetites had been sated and the night plateaued did she have a chance to take a breather by the black marble bar at the back of the room. She noticed Hector clock her and start to make his way through the crowd, before her view of him was blocked by an olive-skinned man holding out his hand and introducing himself as Gennaro Corleone.

He spoke generously, complimenting her effortless handling of guests that evening and ensuring a smooth opening night before speaking of his family's hotel chain in Italy. 'They are not big or fancy,' he said, 'we try for more understated and traditional luxury.'

They welcomed the same faces each season, but what they needed was a new offering and interesting ideas to attract a younger, more affluent audience. The sort of crowd they had welcomed that night at Koyote, and every night in the six weeks since.

At first she was hesitant but there was genuine interest, it seemed, so she spoke briefly about the work she did for Hector – all the while mindful the man in question was about to interrupt at any second. He saw she was on edge, skittish even, and handed her his card as he invited her for coffee the following week.

'I am sure you still have a lot to do tonight, but I would like to talk more. I think you could help me,' he said before making a swift exit.

She pocketed the card quickly as her boss and his bulging forehead vein came up the steps and began to frantically analyse every minute detail of the evening.

Sophie emailed Gennaro the following morning as she nursed a Hector-inspired headache. He'd sent a nineteen-paragraph email at four a.m. with immediate actions and notes for the following day, as if they hadn't hosted their most successful restaurant launch to date. Nothing was good enough. Nothing *she did* was good enough.

Her meeting with Gennaro the following week was pleasant. They sat for two hours in the lobby of the Ace Hotel scribbling excitedly onto notepads as she helped him to flesh out a plan for what he could do with his business. From her bag she produced insights, audience profiles and statistics of where he could learn from competitors and market trends to attract a youthful audience, oblivious to how she was being observed in her element.

If it was intended to be a job interview, she was not aware – but a job offer was what came of it, and she was excited.

She knew that, deep down, Lauren and Craig would be excited too – but first they would need to move past the initial shock of Sophie planning such a drastic life change.

And then there was the Sarah conundrum. Well, the conundrum that currently wasn't, but was about to be, depending on the conversation they were due to have when she arrived in Shepherd's Bush.

Sophie went straight to bed after an uncharacteristically uneventful brunch with Lauren, who had conceded to Sophie's hangover and went back to her beau's flat for another sex marathon.

She spent the following hours oscillating between sleeping and wishing the time away, so she could end the whirlwind of *should-I-or-shouldn't-I* that she didn't have the emotional bandwidth to process.

It was so *deliciously* easy for them to fall back into old habits. Sophie knew she absolutely shouldn't even think about resurrecting her former relationship but that didn't mean it wasn't tempting. The sex was as intense and passionate as it used to be.

She'd forgotten how wonderfully loud Sarah was when she climaxed. Her legs wrapped tight around Sophie's waist, nails clawing at her back and fingers weaved through the roots of her hair. Sophie felt flushed just thinking about it.

The chemistry they shared was quite unlike any she had experienced before, or since. It made it all the more difficult to allow her head to over-rule her heart, or in this case, her clit.

Sarah stood on the corner of Shepherd's Bush Green with the collar of her cream jacket turned up around a beige tartan designer scarf.

She took one look at Sophie and made the executive decision to go for a walk rather than to the pub. Smiling, she looped her arm through Sophie's and led her in the direction of Goldhawk Road.

For a while they strode in a comfortable silence neither was willing to break. The afternoon was turning to evening and the sky full of silver clouds that became greyer and bluer.

The pavements grew wider as they walked down Uxbridge Road. Newly renovated shopfronts turned into upmarket eateries selling burgers as tall as merchant ships. Vegetable vendors packed away their produce in brightly coloured crates, taking them inside while still shouting to flog their last three pounds of potatoes and onions.

Five youths barrelled down the street, stood on the pedals of their bikes and shouting to their friends with the wind in their faces, their navy and grey hoodies catching the wind behind them. *Faster*, they shouted, *faster*, as they dodged the parked cars and wove between buses that honked their horns angrily.

The shops became fewer and the sky became darker. Retailers were replaced by white and beige stone houses three or four floors tall. No longer one single home, they had been divided into anywhere between three and six flats depending on how scrupulous the landlord was.

"Are we going to talk about last night?"

"We should do," Sophie said, unwilling to start the conversation first. She had meticulously combed through every route the conversation could take, envisioning the possible outcomes but was still no clearer on what the best one would be.

"I think you should go first," Sarah said, turning to look at Sophie who was staring at the floor with keen interest. "Look, I know you hate talking about your feelings."

"It's unnecessary..." Sophie muttered.

Because what I want here doesn't actually matter as much as what you want, Sophie thought.

"It's good practice for you," Sarah prompted. "You're not dead inside."

And I know you aren't, Sarah continued in her head, *because I've spent the last twenty months thinking about how heartbroken your face was when I ended things between us.*

A pang of guilt wrung her insides and rose to sting the backs of her eyes. *No, no, now Sarah, you can't go crying before you've even had words. Come on now, pull yourself together.*

"This is complicated. *We* are complicated," Sophie said.

"I hope you're not going to continue stating the obvious."

Sophie said nothing as she tried to make sense of how she felt. Feelings always complicated matters once spoken aloud, and she could not recount a single instance when doing so improved any situation.

The truth was, they were always difficult to decode in the moment. It was only days or even weeks after the fact, when she had lain in bed with nothing but the darkness for company, that she understood how she felt and why.

Usually by then it was too late to do anything about it.

Complicating matters further was Sarah's penchant for producing a one-second psychoanalysis of every sentence, poking and prodding at each word to gauge its true meaning, leading Sophie to tie herself in knots.

"Okay. I'll go first," Sarah said. "I honestly didn't intend for anything more than a friendly drink to happen between us. I swear it. While what happened was unexpected... I enjoyed it."

Sophie remained pensive.

"Ahh, look. You know, in the run-up to the wedding with Chris, I came to realise that I ran to him because I was running away from something else. And I was too late to do anything about it, like the stupid idiot that I am. You're right, we are complicated. But does that mean... does that mean... that we shouldn't?"

Sophie's mind flickered back to the dull thud of her stomach dropping, her eyes burning and her head buried deep in her pillow after deleting Sarah's number. What followed was four hours of intense gardening that began at seven in the morning and ended in her falling asleep, exhausted, in a deck chair by eleven.

Craig called her Butch Billy for a week. He'd never seen her in overalls before.

She played out the memory of them for weeks after. Imagining conversations that would never happen. Resolving that if they were to meet again, and the opportunity to speak presented itself, she would tell Sarah exactly how she felt.

But she didn't.

Too much time had passed and those words felt meaningless now.

"You were difficult to get over," Sophie began hesitantly. "Because... I suppose... well, for the first time in a long time, I felt like I was involved in something that had potential. You seemed to really like me, and you're funny, you're clever, and you even laugh when I tell you a story I've told you twice before."

"I couldn't stop thinking about you. I still can't, Sophie," Sarah whispered so quietly that the words were almost taken by the wind.

Sophie took a second.

"There hasn't been anybody of consequence. Not since you," she replied. "I know we were never supposed to be anything, but I still felt like an idiot when it ended."

"And now?"

"Now I don't know how I feel. I want to, but I don't think it's a good idea."

They took a left down Askew Road and towards Ravenscourt Park. The houses-cum-flats were different now, shorter and stubbier; the end of Shepherd's Bush that nobody really wanted to live in until house prices rocketed and anywhere in Zone 2 or 3 was an investment with infinite reward. The terraces with patchwork rendering, some polished and pristine, some with the plaster chipped and dull, picked out the older inhabitants from the new.

"I cannot stress enough how incredibly sorry I am for hurting you, Sophie." Sarah stopped walking and took both of her hands in the empty street. "I was a coward. I was scared of what dating a woman meant."

"But you actively looked to date a woman. You found me on Bumble."

"I know, I know, but when push came to shove... I... I was terrified. I didn't know what I wanted. I am getting on a bit, you know. You're young, you–"

"Don't play the age card."

Sarah looked to the floor and smiled. "It took almost marrying the wrong person to realise that I shouldn't have discounted somebody who was a much better fit for me than Chris ever was."

"What do you want from me?"

"I want us to start again, if you'll have me."

"I'm not a rebound."

"You're never, ever going to be a rebound for me. You should have been my first choice. My only choice." Sarah brushed at the parting which had formed a large V in Sophie's otherwise straight fringe. "I get it's a lot to ask, and if you're not comfortable..."

Oh bollocks. Lauren really was going to go ballistic.

Chapter Ten

The oak dining table was covered in paper fall-out. Invoices littered every surface, which she would have to pay regardless of whether she'd walked down the aisle or not.

In the four weeks since the wedding-that-wasn't, she found herself fobbing off friends left, right and centre who wanted to hear the story from the horse's mouth.

Sarah was convinced that Aoife, Morag, her mother, Caro and Fiona had a schedule between them that determined who would call and when to check up on her. She had heard third-hand from one of them, but which one she wasn't so sure, that Chris had cancelled their honeymoon and taken himself to New Zealand, followed by a fortnight with his parents in Limerick before landing back in London three days prior.

Good for him, she thought. The last thing she wanted was for him to come back immediately and hole himself up in the flat for weeks on end, though who was she to voice an opinion on what he chose to do any more? If she wanted to do that then she should have married him.

Helen bounced down the stairs and into the kitchen in full running attire. She was Australian, as tall as Sophie, a good foot taller than Sarah, with a broader, more muscular frame and black hair tied back into a bun on the crown of her head.

She was a near-stranger to her, having only met her twice after answering a SpareRoom advert and being the only potential flatmate she met who did not give her the creeps. It transpired that they had a lot in common, mainly the appreciation of Savignon Blanc and binge-watching boxsets on a Friday night.

"Do you want me to bring back anything?" Helen said.

"If you find my sanity out there, please return it. Other than that, I'm all good." Sarah let out a heavy breath and dejectedly stared at the sea of white paper.

"OK, I'll bring back some wine for tonight. What time are you meeting Chris?"

Sarah had been riddled with anxiety since he left an abrupt voicemail asking to meet. He cared not for her time and gave her no option to meet anywhere else other than at three p.m. on Putney High Street.

It was a miserable day. The sun had absconded, leaving heavy grey clouds that grew darker until the rain came down across London with such ferocity that even the foxes took shelter. Lights from shopfronts were reflected in large puddles gathered on the pavements, and streams ran hurriedly down the street before being snatched by storm drains.

The thick mist of rain clung to her like a second skin as her feet pounded the pavements. She spotted the café at the end of their old street and made a run for it.

Chris was by the window with his back to the door. He was staring to the street, but with such darkness outside, the only thing he could see was the reflection of himself. He had caught a tan in the infancy of spring in New Zealand.

Sarah found herself standing by the table and holding her breath until he drew his attention from the past and into the present, where they were together for the first time since they kissed goodnight after the rehearsal dinner.

"I'm so, so sorry, Chris. I–"

"Save it, Sarah. I don't want to hear it. I'm here to find out why."

A lump grew in her throat. She exhaled forcefully to steady herself and took a seat in the blue plastic chair opposite.

"I've done a lot of thinking... and my reaction was wrong. Totally wrong. It was also wrong of me to let it go that far... when I started to get doubts, I should have done something then."

"So what were your doubts? I don't get it, Sarah. I looked..." he faltered, "I looked an absolute fucking fool."

She drew her lips in further until they were no longer plump and pink but a thin line.

"I'm sorry."

"I'll tell you what I need. I don't need you to keep saying you're sorry, I need you to help me to understand," he hissed, leaning forward and placing his hands on the table before retreating back into himself to avoid drawing attention.

The café was only half full.

Most people were alone at their laptops sporting large headphones, there for the cheap coffee which kept them fuelled through long days and longer nights. The rest were families with large buggies seeking shelter from the rain and a warm drink to bring the feeling back to their fingers.

"You're such a kind, kind man. And I honestly think that we wanted – want – the same things. I just don't think that you are the right person for me to pursue them with."

"What? How did you only realise that the morning of the wedding? Is there someone else?"

"Yes. No. I don't know. *I don't know* how it took me so long to realise."

"Yes, there's someone else?" Chris asked incredulously.

"No, no there isn't." Sarah paused and massaged her temples. "I rushed into it. I think we were both guilty of getting swept up in building a future without considering if we were really doing it with the right person."

"Can I ask, did you cheat on me?"

"What? No, no, of course not. I'm not that much of a raging bitch."

"Debatable," he quipped under his breath.

"Oh, for fuck's sake," Sarah said.

"No, I'm sorry. I'm just – I'm just struggling to process everything but I think you're right. Not, you know, about running off but that we were chasing after a future too soon..."

"What I did to you was... was unforgivable. I cannot apologise enough. You never have to see me again." They both stared at the table in a stilted silence. "You'll find someone, someone much better than me. I promise."

She instinctively reached over the table to take hold of his hand but then withdrew.

"I think you should go."

Sarah took the long route home. She didn't deserve the convenience of an Uber.

She would have found herself in this situation sooner or later whether she had Sophie in her past, or present, or not. It would have just taken her longer to realise that she was pursuing the right things with the wrong person.

But how wrong was he, really? Surely not so wrong that she only realised at the last minute she had his whole heart, but he didn't have hers.

She could have been settled in the sort of relationship she grew up dreaming of well into adulthood.

And that's what it would have been; settling. Sure, she would not have been the only woman in the world to be loved more than she loved in return, but that was surely preferable to if the situation was reversed.

Wasn't it?

All things considered, she would have been as happy as she could have been with everything she thought she wanted. They'd have the house, children – hopefully – and a perfectly content life together where she wouldn't have to worry about very much at all.

How careless to have all that ready for her and to throw it away. Ghastly, even.

Selfish rotten bitch.

And what of Sophie, where did she fit? Sarah wasn't sure. All she knew was that, with her, she felt at peace. Her mind was quiet, as if they were only the two people in the world who mattered.

There were no opinions shared by those on the outside looking in. No parents, in-laws, sisters, brothers, nieces or nephews, or the butcher's brother's wife adding her two cents in. No opinions mattered but theirs; there were no expectations to conform to.

How it would evolve was hard to say. Their bubble felt comfortably uncomplicated, despite the situation being anything but.

It wasn't love. Maybe it could be, but now they were happy meandering along in the company of each other with no plan beyond the present and no pressure to be anything more than they were. Anything that happened would be purely organic, if anything happened at all, and she was happy to wait and see.

Chapter Eleven

"Sarah, your phone is going mad down here," Helen shouted up the stairs of their two-bed maisonette, her voice ricocheting off oak laminate floors and clinical white walls.

"Sarah McCarthy, I think you have some explaining to do!" Caroline barked down the phone as soon as it was answered.

"I'm sorry, what now?" Sarah said, mouthing *thanks* to Helen who handed her a glass of wine.

"Did you leave Chris for someone else?"

"What? No! Where did you get this from?"

"But you met Chris this afternoon, correct?"

"Yes, but I–"

"And you said there was someone else?"

"No, no this isn't true. Where the feck has this come from?"

"Chris spoke to Michael, Michael called Morag and Morag called me to see if I knew anything."

"Jesus wept," she retorted, "I've only been home a couple of hours and suddenly Cork is alight with gossip. Chris got the wrong end of the stick two hours ago and I set him right. Why he's gone and told Michael that, I don't know."

Caroline made a disapproving nasal noise down the phone.

"Sorry now, what is it you want me to do? Give him a hard time for talking shite like he hasn't had enough of a hard time because of me?"

"Yes, but Sarah…"

"No, do you know what?" Sarah cut off her sister, "I've had enough already. Good luck and fuck ye."

Sarah raised the bottom of her glass and took the drink in one. Helen looked on, bemused. Sarah was shaking with anger. Did her sister seriously believe there was a breath of truth in it? Did she think so little of her?

As if leaving the poor creature at the altar wasn't enough, to tell him there was another man not even a month later was sheer cruelty. And the fact was, there wasn't a man.

But a woman, perhaps… said the back of her mind and so she felt a pang of guilt, though not just for that.

Perhaps she shouldn't have told Caroline to get fucked either.

19:07: Caroline – I'm sorry, I thought it was ridiculous really. I didn't mean to accuse you of cheating. Friends?

19:08: Sarah – I'm sorry I said what I did.

19:10: Caroline – Have a glass of wine and chill out tonight. Nobody seriously believes it, I think that's why they were shocked. I'll speak to Michael. Love you x

Helen topped up Sarah's glass, knowing it wouldn't be long before they were opening another and sharing a cigarette under the bay window.

The Irishwoman had her elbows on the table with her head in her hands. Helen didn't want to pry, but she did want to know who she was effing and blinding at down the phone. She'd tell her, in good time, perhaps when she saw the bottom of her third glass.

Sarah picked up her phone to text Sophie.

20:03: Sarah – I wish you were here x

Here beside me, on my sofa, with my head resting in the nook of your neck.

Sarah knew that there would come a point where telling Helen about Sophie was a logistical necessity. The few nights she and Sophie had spent together in the past month were at Sophie's flat where she narrowly avoided being detected by Craig, or in hotels she couldn't justify paying for among the invoices for the wedding.

It would also be nice, she thought, for somebody she knew to be privy to the significant secret she had been keeping.

She hadn't known Helen for long enough to worry a great deal about judgement that may or may not come. Though she was pretty sure that Helen wouldn't cast any. In the month they had lived together, she realised how unlike her friends the Australian was.

Helen was free-spirited in a way Sarah found genuinely refreshing. She was a little too much of everything – sometimes too loud, too crass, too tipsy, too confident, but at the same time, completely aware of herself and unapologetic about it.

What she lacked was any worry about shame, and deep down, Sarah wished she had a little of that too.

She also found herself wishing that she could talk to Aoife or Morag, but not enough to actually do it. That was a conversation best avoided until she knew what exactly was happening. If she'd ever want to have it at all, she'd brought enough shame to her family already.

Chapter Twelve

"**Y**ou've put a gun to my head here, Sophie. I don't appreciate this."

"Honestly, Hector, I'm not doing it on purpose. We've been taking reservations for opening night for almost two months! We can't cancel those now."

"But something is *wrong,*" he stressed.

"Three extra light fittings is not a constitutional emergency."

She could imagine him at the other end, his face flushed purple with the vein pulsating with a life of its own.

"The builders should be paying for the corrections."

"But it's not their fault." *It's yours, you daft prick.* Sophie paced back and forth in the barren office to keep herself grounded and her voice level. She was running late for dinner with Craig. They'd planned to visit their favourite Thai restaurant, Jasmine Dreams, and if she didn't end the conversation she wouldn't make it at all with the way Hector was carrying on. Everybody in the team had left over an hour ago.

"But why can't they pay it?"

Deep breath, Sophie. You are calm, content, Zen. A godly presence with no ill-feeling towards the blundering idiot at the end of the phone. Babbling brooks, floating clouds, fields of wheat blowing in a gentle breeze. She opened her eyes and exhaled.

"Hector," Sophie said, firmly regretting the moment she signed her contract. "On the fourteenth of May, you signed off on the restaurant plans. You specifically asked for the light fittings to be in one single line, no more than six bulbs, above the counter. You, with a blue biro pen, which I remember because it leaked in your trouser pocket and sent me to the cleaners instead of Ana because you didn't trust her to do it, signed those designs. We cannot now, on the seventh of November, change those plans when you've had the entire site re-wired and released the money for the fit-out because you now want only three lightbulbs."

Close your eyes and think of Italy. No, wait, don't think of Italy because you're not going. You're staying in London to work things out with your sort-of-ex-girlfriend, and no, she doesn't know you've pressed pause on la dolce vita *for her. Yes, think of Sarah. Think of the duck spring rolls you're going to eat for dinner. You are calm, a Zen goddess.*

"But we have too many lights."

"Goodnight, Hector, I shall see you on Monday." Sophie hung up.

He'd be absolutely raging and would no doubt call her into the office on Monday morning to give her a bollocking. *Sod him,* she thought, *let him rage. I bet he'll have come back around to his original idea of six and be walking around on Monday thinking he's the next intellectual mastermind, taking an online test for Mensa, which he'd no doubt fail and be back to sulking like a miserable bastard.*

Sophie took a running kick at a wastepaper basket and looked up towards the door onto the street to find Craig peering through the other side. "Two seconds," she mouthed to him and held up two fingers before grabbing her bag and running out of the door.

"Who riled you up so much?"

"Who do you think?"

"The purple shouty man."

"Exactly."

"Beer?" Craig lifted the flap of his tan leather satchel to produce two bottles of Peroni and cracked the lids off with the bottle opener he kept on his keys. The slender, bearded man cocked one eyebrow as she looked at him, astounded.

"Where did they come from and how are they cold?" Sophie laughed, crossing the road and heading for Soho.

"Never you mind and ice-packs." He smiled. "So what's new? I feel like it's been ages since we've done anything together."

"I know," Sophie mused. "I feel like my life is more dull without your bright wardrobe being as frequent. Have you been with your fancy man?"

"Well, yes, I was. Until his wife came home and found us in bed together."

"You're joking!" Sophie said incredulously.

"Another one bites the dust," Craig sighed.

Sophie offered her bottle up for a cheers.

They cut down the side of Liberty towards Carnaby Street; its Christmas lights were still unlit for another two weeks, a fact which didn't seem to deter tourists from stopping in the street with their cameras aloft. She and Craig split up to negotiate the pushing and shoving of the Friday crowds and after-work drinkers.

Sophie noticed a woman in an expensive khaki coat holding a dog which looked more like a rat, barking incessantly at the crowds. She grew agitated in her attempts to calm him down. 'He doesn't like crowds,' she told her friend, who did not look amused. She was undoubtedly wondering why the furry thing had been brought to Central London in the first place.

They emerged from the ruckus on Beak Street and headed east towards Soho. Passing queues outside walk-in-only restaurants and people spilling out of pubs, onto pavements, onto roads, all for the sake of having a drink without somebody putting their elbow in their pint.

"Now I have your ear… I know it's not been Katie that's keeping you busy. So who is?" Craig said with a smile playing on his lips.

"Do you have another beer?"

"Stop changing the subject. You aren't good at it."

"Ahhh," Sophie said. "You're not going to be pleased to know, it's Sarah."

"Sophie!" Craig stopped still and stamped his foot petulantly. Some stopped and turned their heads to the man in the red trousers. "We have talked about this. Does Lauren know?"

"*No!* Of course she doesn't. You're the only one I've told."

"Well. I can't deny that I'm happy I know something she doesn't for a change, but I am very disappointed in you."

"And that's not all."

"You mean there's more?"

She'd said too much, it was the beer. Sophie should have kept it to herself but while they were sharing and while she had the courage, she went all in.

"I've had a job offer to work at a hotel chain… in Italy. But I'm not going, not yet, I don't think…"

"But what about Sarah?" he asked.

"Oh, so now you're concerned about me leaving her?"

"No, yes… I don't know if I should be encouraging you to go and bin her off or stay in London for purely selfish reasons," said Craig. "I don't like Sarah, Lauren doesn't either. Yes, you should go to Italy and forget about her. Oh, I don't know. I'm terribly conflicted and this is all too much." Craig dashed off down the pavement for dramatic effect. She indulged him briefly before he allowed her to catch up. "What did you say to the job offer?"

"I said I'd need six months to figure this out, and then he'd have my answer."

"Six months is punchy."

"He said to take my time, so I am. You never know, I could end up there."

Chapter Thirteen

Legend had it – and it was only so because Sophie herself publicised it – that Boozy Lauren could be summoned at any point by walking into a pub, looking in a mirror with a drink in hand and chanting 'Boozy Lauren, Boozy Lauren, Boozy Lauren.' Then as if by magic, the woman herself would appear behind you, sporting an impish grin and a pint of beer like Beetlejuice.

It was a day that began in a damp and drizzly fashion. A fine mist of rain clung to London only to be burnt away by the winter sun that bore a blue-skied afternoon. Sceptical Londoners – as most were – still clung to their umbrellas. A man raised his as a woman lowered hers and they passed without incident.

December dawned, marked by the traditional flurry of holiday party invites and twinkling lights down Regent Street. Optimistic Christmas shoppers tackled Oxford Street with gusto and booking a table for dinner in any restaurant became nightmarish unless you wanted to dine out on a Monday.

For the first time since Maria and Kirsten's wedding two months ago, she and Lauren we reunited with the lovebirds.

When Sophie told people she was the maid of honour at the wedding of two of her exes, people thought she was joking. Unless the person she was telling also happened to be sapphically-inclined, then they understood completely and it needed no further explanation.

The story perhaps was embellished slightly. She was absolutely their maid of honour and she had slept with them both, multiple times, but they were not *officially* exes. They had friend-zoned each other before anything really established itself, so when they entered a relationship with each other, there was no drama to be had.

Femmes were not easy to spot in the wild, so she and Maria had met on a dating app. She had met Kirsten at a corporate hospitality event two years later. Then Maria and Kirsten had met each other at Sophie's birthday drinks and hit it off right away.

Lauren joined the fray in a purely platonic way and they had remained a foursome ever since. That night they gathered in Sophie's poky kitchen enjoying the finest Pinot Noir the local supermarket had to offer.

The coating was peeling from the laminate floors and the cream vinyl of the nineties kitchen had been scratched by a revolving door of tenants who had called this ground-floor flat home over the past ten years.

Skirting boards didn't quite meet the sloping floors in a landlord-special DIY extension; one which saw the lounge pushed into the garden so the room by the front door could be turned into an extra bedroom.

Sophie had shifted the table from the wall into the middle of the room to allow just enough space for four seats around the edges, and four risotto-filled bowls thereon.

"I'm sorry, can we just take a moment to say I cannot believe you've kept all of this a secret for almost three months?" asked Maria. "And you didn't even tell Lauren?"

"Yes, well, I knew she'd go mad. Didn't I?" Sophie said, casting a sideways glance at the woman in question who sat cross-legged on the sagging leather sofa.

"And did she?"

"Yes, actually. She hit me with a ring-binder and didn't speak to me for two days."

Sophie knew she had to tell Lauren and the longer she left it, the more upset her best friend would become. She decided that she might soften the blow by treating them to fondue and wine at the Carlton Terrace on Marylebone High Street, but her ruse was quickly dashed.

She listened in rapt fascination as her Lauren recounted her most recent date with the assistant manager of the skincare shop on Hampstead High Street. They went back to his place and as she waited in his room for him to freshen up, her eyes landed on a stack of children's books by his bed.

With absolutely no other evidence at all, she decided the man must be a paedophile and started to panic. He returned to Lauren frantically trying to wiggle into her skinny jeans, almost toppling over into his bedside table.

Had she waited a little longer for the explanation that eventually came, she would have been reassured to learn he was the author of said books, and so she stayed. All was well in the world again, or so she thought, until he was on the cusp of orgasm and started quoting Shakespeare.

"On the bright side, better a poet than a paedo," Sophie said.

Lauren smiled but she smelled a rat.

Sophie's conversation was stilted, her sentences short and sharp enough to kill a man. The waiter had no sooner placed fresh wine glasses on the table before Lauren launched into an interrogation that would put Cromwell to shame.

Forlorn wasn't the right word for how Lauren looked on learning of Sophie's secret affair. She looked at her friend with a mix of disdain and exasperation, mildly thankful that Sophie had the decency to look sheepish.

There were no assurances that Sophie could give about her and Sarah that would quell the rumbling suspicion she felt inside.

It didn't matter to her that they were taking it slow, they hadn't put a label on it or were deeply enamoured with each other. All she knew is that it would all end in tears, for Sarah wouldn't risk the shame of coming out to her family.

She also failed to believe Sophie when she said it didn't matter to her that Sarah wasn't or may never come out, or that she hadn't pinned any hopes on her wanting to be in a long-term relationship.

What did come as even more of a shock, and she had to stop herself physically kicking Sophie in the shins, was to learn that her friend had a once-in-a-lifetime job offer and hadn't bit Gennaro's hand off to take it.

If she didn't care that much about the potential of the Irishwoman then she would have done so.

That was the difficult thing with being friends with Sophie. She said one thing but her actions betrayed her, even if she wasn't emotionally astute to recognise the link between the two; so Lauren stayed silent.

The best thing she could do was to continue that silence, for the most part anyway, and allow the situation to organically unfold into terrible heartbreak or blissful against-the-odds happiness. There was no telling in which direction they might go, but she would certainly be there at the end to find out.

But she may, once or twice, vocalise her disapproval just to remind Sophie of her stance on the situation.

"OK, so – Sophie's telling us she and Sarah are semi-casual," Lauren said to Maria and Kirsten. "Now, Soph, tell them about your trip to the theatre last weekend."

Sophie looked over at Lauren.

"So last Saturday," Sophie began, looking over to see if Lauren was going to tag-team with her on the story she already knew, "I bought myself a ticket to the theatre. I had planned on going home because Sarah was taking me out for dinner and drinks on the Saturday, then just as the curtain went up, I get this text…"

19:25: Sarah – Hey, how's the theatre? Do you want to come here when you're finished? I've made spud bolognese. No worries if you've already got plans though… x

19:32 – Sophie: I'm not going to question the spud bolognese but that'll need explaining to me. What's wrong with pasta? Will text you when I leave. x

19:45 – Sarah: Can't wait x

And from that moment her solo date night was overtaken by thoughts of her not-girlfriend.

While they had been dating for months by now, they held an unspoken and mutually acknowledged wariness about what sort of future they had and so keenly avoided any discussion of official labels or plans too far into the future for fear of upsetting the applecart.

The wariness paled in comparison to the depth of their entrancement with one another.

There was a fifty-fifty chance of things going well or 'tits up' as Lauren so deftly put it. The way Sophie saw it was, if they didn't work then she could never say they didn't try. On the other, if they did work, they'd be able to work through anything else life threw at them.

But on the bright side, if she did end up miserable then she would rather be so in Italy than London. And the thought of a Mediterranean brunette to take her mind off things wasn't a bad one at all.

And then she felt a pang of guilt for even considering that as a potential part of her future when she was so happy in her present.

The complexities of their situation were often overwhelming, so Sophie had established the habit of shutting down any consideration of them before they got too far. It was wise, in her opinion, to let Sarah lead their dance and go with wherever it took them.

If she expected nothing, then she couldn't be disappointed. Sound logic, surely?

Sophie found herself on the doorstep of Sarah's Wandsworth maisonette before the curtain even fell on the play. She had left at the interval; the logical part of her brain scolded her for the waste of both money and opportunity, but she ignored it as she had recently become accustomed to doing.

Sarah answered the door quickly, pink-cheeked and red-eyed with a glass of Sauvignon Blanc in hand. She paused for a moment before leading Sophie into the flat, taking a seat on a cushion already positioned under the bay window propped open by a wine bottle, and lit a cigarette. The night air crept in and snatched the silver swirls of smoke away.

Sarah took a deep and unsteady breath and for a moment Sophie believed that everything was about to be over.

"Why have you been crying, Sarah?" Sophie knelt down and brushed a stray curl back from Sarah's damp face.

"I had a massive heart-to-heart with Helen tonight."

"I see..." Sophie said, hoping Sarah would continue unprompted.

"I told her about... about us." She grimaced and nodded her head definitively.

"And... what is it about that conversation that upset you? Did she not take it well?"

"I just thought she'd hate me."

"Oh, Sarah," said Sophie, as Sarah pulled her in close.

"And I…" Sarah spoke into her chest. "I asked if it was all right, that you could come around and stay here sometimes. And she said… she said of course. Oh, she was so lovely."

Sarah sniffed.

"Well, that's a good thing, I suppose. We can't afford so many hotels." Sophie tried to raise a smile, but the joke sunk like a steel Birkenstock in a paddling pool.

"I don't know what I'm doing, Sophie."

"I can't tell you what to do, love." She cupped Sarah's face and watched as she relaxed into her.

"I know it's hard and the best we can do is take our time. This is our business and ours alone."

Sarah turned her head to kiss Sophie's palm and smile.

"But I'm not gay. I don't know what I am."

"You don't need to label yourself."

Sarah lay with her head on Sophie's shoulder and for a while they sat against the wall in comfortable silence with their fingers woven and legs locked together. In the moments between the darkness and her dreams, Sarah had mulled over the imagined reactions from her friends and family to her relationship with the younger woman.

There she would be, in the sitting room of her parents' house on the hill, staring too hard at the narrow hedgerow-lined track that ran down to Lough Mahon. Nameless faces who could easily be substituted for her mother/father/sisters/Aoife/Morag (delete as appropriate), for they would all react in the same manner, she supposed, updating her on daily life in Cork.

She wouldn't be listening. She'd open her mouth, lose the words and close it again. The person to her right would notice after the third attempt and lean forward with serious concern.

No, she wasn't ill, she'd say. *No, my finances are fine, my house is fine, my friends are fine. It's... I'm... in a relationship with a woman. She's wonderful, so kind... called Sophie... yes, yes I'm serious. She's twenty-nine. Yes, that's almost a ten-year difference, I know, but... we don't notice it at all. But... please will you just let me speak? I know what you're thinking but she's not like that, not at all. She's a good job, she lives in London too and we're... we're good together. Why... why don't you understand? No, Mam, please don't cry. Dad, look at me please. It's not a midlife crisis. I'm sorry. I'm so sorry, I never wanted to hurt you, hurt any of you. Please don't hate me. Please.*

No matter how many times she practiced the conversation in her head, it always went the same way, and like falling down a step on the cusp of sleep, she would jolt awake.

The thing was, she knew her parents had no problem with gay people. Caro's best friend was gay and when he came home from Mykonos with a wooden cock-shaped bottle opener as a present for their Mam, she thought it was a riot, and had produced it from the kitchen at every opportunity since.

She was never, she would never, ever say anything to anybody about their sexuality.

But her own daughter? That would be different.

Her thirty-nine-year-old daughter who had never given her any cause to think she was anything other than straight.

How happy Finnoula was when Sarah rang home to announce her engagement to Chris. If that name had been switched to Sophie, or any other female name for that matter, she'd hate it. She was sure of it. Oh, it would be horrible.

Then the talk. Not only did Sarah McCarthy do a runner at her own wedding, did you hear she was now a *lesbian,* they would whisper in hushed tones. Except she wasn't a lesbian, she didn't know what she was – not that the gossipmongers would care.

And it would be her parents who bore the brunt of those with small minds and large mouths. They'd talk and gossip in the pub or the shop and fall silent when Finnoula or Fred walked by, exchanging side-eyed looks as if to say 'there they go, the parents of that Sarah who ditched her fiancé and took up with another woman.'

If she announced she was with a woman, or 'came out', she'd be forcing one shameful event atop another on her parents who didn't deserve the attention it would bring to their family.

And that thought terrified her.

Anyway, was she really 'coming out'? It wasn't as if she had a history of being with women. Looking back on her colourful sexual and romantic history, sure, maybe she'd fallen into bed with women a couple of times, but it always been men she felt drawn to, whether sober or drunk.

She'd looked at women before when they got on the bus, or the Tube, or walked in front of her in the supermarket. She'd noticed their shoes, or their skirt or their bag, and she'd wonder where they were from.

They may be pretty in the face, but she didn't want to kiss them. They had a great bum sometimes, great legs, but she didn't admire them like that.

It was only Sophie. It was only ever Sophie.

The way her skin glowed even in the morning and her smile shone to make her forget the worst of days, the hourglass figure she always had the urge to run her hands over, the fullness of her chest that Sarah pressed her cheeks against. It was only Sophie who made her feel the way she did.

But she categorically wasn't gay. Not even bisexual. And whatever she *was*, nobody could know. Not yet anyway. And there was a part of her still unsure if anybody could ever know.

Sophie awoke in the dead of night to the door of the flat slamming shut and somebody tap-dancing across the wooden floor.

The heels of Helen's shoes clattered noisily for a few minutes before coming to a standstill when she noticed the lamp was still on and two pairs of feet were dangling over the arm of the sofa.

Through bleary eyes, Sophie saw two tanned hands appear on the back of the chair before a face riddled with confusion peered over the top. Helen's hair was jet black and scraped into a messy bun atop her head. Her smile lines stretched down her cheeks as she grinned at the women half-asleep before her.

Earlier that evening, the Australian had been sworn to secrecy as Sarah sat on the sofa hopelessly sobbing, and ever since, she had been desperate to know more about her housemate's secret girlfriend. Though if she was honest, she had been expecting somebody rather... different.

That's what lesbians did, right? There was a feminine one, which was Sarah, so the other one had to be more... you know – buzzcut and bootcuts. More masculine. Right?

But no, Sarah was cuddled into the neck of a woman very feminine indeed. Pale. British, undoubtedly so. And... staring right back at her.

Helen reached for the light.

"Ah, for fuck's sake now, Helen," Sarah said, her voice laced with sleep. "Are ye going to stand there all night?"

"Are you Sophie?" said the Australian excitedly. "You don't look how I imagined."

"Dare I ask what you were expecting?"

"Best not," she replied. "Shall I get us a glass of wine?"

"What time is it?" Sarah yawned.

"It's only one o'clock. C'mon now, let's have a drink."

Chapter Fourteen

The promise of Christmas hung heavy in the air and festive lights twinkled in the mist that had set over the city.

A blustery wind rippled the surface of puddles that gathered in the pavement crevices. Sophie stood in the shadows of East London's past, on damp streets lined by red-bricked Georgian terraces. It was their last night together before they returned home for Christmas; Sarah to Ireland for the first time since the-wedding-that-wasn't and Sophie to Manchester.

The door she faced looked more like a bank safe than one to a restaurant. If she hadn't known a Michelin star lay at the other side then she would never have guessed it was the entrance to a place where people would actively want to spend an evening, and pay handsome money for the pleasure.

The maître d' welcomed her with a smile that did not reach her eyes and took her coat to hang in a mahogany wardrobe, then passed her to a server who would take her to Sarah.

Fashionably low lights hung above circular tables set back into cave-like dining booths. Expensive bottles of wine stood to attention facing label-out.

If Sophie's years in hospitality had taught her anything, it was to expect the unexpected. Though she couldn't quite grasp the logic of placing a rickety rope bridge between an artificial rock gorge separating one part of the restaurant from the other. How many plates of food had been dropped over the edge when there was only enough space for one person at a time to cross?

It was an extravagant space with superficial novelty and most definitely designed by a man, Sophie decided, because a woman would have thought of the logistics of crossing said bridge wearing a pair of stilettos.

"I've already told the waiter that we'll only need one dessert menu later." Sarah grinned after placing a light kiss on the corner of Sophie's mouth. "You look wonderful tonight, my love."

"You are also looking delightful." Sophie squeezed her hand as she took her seat.

Candlelight caught the contours of Sarah's cheeks which became rounder as she smiled.

"Helen is going to meet us for a drink after dinner. She'll want to go to Soho, is that OK?"

"Of course, I've not been to Soho in ages," said Sophie.

"I'm sorry, you know, about last night." Sarah began, her voice barely above a whisper. She fiddled with the hem of her shirt, avoiding Sophie's gaze. "I just need you to understand that I can't tell anybody else, not yet. I need to understand myself first."

The words hung in the air between them. Sophie felt a familiar ache in her chest.

"Sarah, it's not the end of the world. Honestly, I get it. I've been there," Sophie said, remembering the near-universal anxiety that came with acknowledging that she wasn't entirely straight. In fact, she was most definitely fully homosexual.

The realisation had hit her like an epiphany. She was sixteen and staring a little bit too hard at a photo of Cheryl Cole by the pool on holiday. The glossy magazine page had crinkled under her sweaty fingertips as she'd tried to make sense of the flutter in her stomach and the heat rising to her cheeks.

Sarah looked up, a hint of curiosity breaking through her worried expression. "How... how did you know? For sure, I mean."

Sophie paused, choosing her words carefully. "It wasn't like a lightning bolt, you know? More like... putting on glasses for the first time. Suddenly, all these little moments from my life came into focus. The 'girl crushes' that were definitely more than admiration, the way I'd always notice women and men would never even register on my radar. Fancying my PE teacher though should have been a dead giveaway though."

She trailed off, noticing Sarah's intense gaze. "But everyone's journey is different, love. There's no rush, no timeline you have to follow."

Sarah nodded slowly, her shoulders relaxing a fraction. "It's just... I keep imagining telling my parents. In my head, it always ends in tears and disappointment. I've already shamed them enough. I can't do it again."

"Take your time, Sarah. We're in this together, yeah? No pressure, no expectations. Just us, figuring it out day by day."

Sarah squeezed Sophie's hand, her eyes shining with unshed tears and something that looked a lot like hope. "Thank you," she whispered, leaning in to rest her forehead against Sophie's.

And for a moment, everything felt possible.

The two women stepped out into the brisk winter night, their breath forming misty clouds in the air. Helen strode confidently down the street, a striking figure in her all-black ensemble of boots, jeans, and a leather jacket.

Tonight felt different. Something had shifted between her and Sarah. There was a new sense of purpose, of intent, that hadn't existed before, though Sophie wondered if it might just be the wine clouding her judgement.

As they navigated the warren-like streets of Soho, Sophie reflected on her early days in London. A decade ago, she couldn't have found her way through these streets sober if her life depended on it. But give her three vodka tonics, and suddenly every shop front, bar, and alleyway became as familiar as the back of her hand. The memory brought a wry smile to her face as they descended the dark steps under UV lights into one of Soho's few late-night gay clubs.

Inside, the room pulsed with energy. Men in tight black pants served drinks and danced on the bar under flashing lights. Sophie watched in amusement as Helen's eyes scanned the room with hawk-like precision, quickly arming herself with a double gin before making a beeline for the only straight man in sight – a talent Sophie had previously thought unique to Lauren.

As they sipped vodkas through thin straws in thick plastic glasses, Sophie found herself caught in the swirl of clammy bodies writhing to R&B. Hands pushed and grabbed in the crowd, creating a stop-motion effect under the strobe lights. Sarah wrapped her arms around Sophie's neck in a rare but confident display of public affection, drawing her in for a leisurely kiss that left Sophie's heart racing.

When Sarah returned from the bar with fresh drinks, Sophie found herself mesmerised. Sarah stood still for a moment, head slightly downcast, lips as red as Sophie's own wrapped around her straw. The black jumpsuit with its teasing V-neck hinted at a cleavage that Sophie found delightful. As Sarah noticed her staring, a coy smile spread across her face, reaching her bright, beaming eyes. Time stood still, and they were the only two people in the room.

And that's when it hit her.

"Fuck," she thought, "I'm in love with Sarah."

The epiphany was both thrilling and terrifying. This wasn't supposed to happen. Love meant Italy was off the cards. Love meant the potential for heartbreak. Love meant there was more at stake should Sarah not feel the same way.

But love shouldn't have come as a surprise at all.

As the implications cascaded through her mind, Sophie could only think one thing:

Oh bloody bollocks arsehole tit wank fart.

Love had struck Sophie before, but it had always been fleeting, leaving behind more hurt than harmony. She decided it could all be fine, so long as she kept quiet about it. This was on revelation best kept to herself, Sarah might run a mile otherwise. Anyway, she wasn't entirely if this new feeling was the result of mixing wine and vodka in the same evening.

"Are you ready to go?" A cool hand on her back jolted Sophie from her thoughts. "I think Helen's on the verge of being kicked out for mounting that poor creature," Sarah said, nodding towards Helen's conquest.

They squeezed clumsily into a taxi – four adults instead of three, as Helen had invited the man home. Sophie didn't feel sorry for him any more. The Kiwi, whom they'd dubbed 'Keith' (though neither Sarah nor Sophie was sure of his actual name), was glued to Helen by the lips.

Sophie sat in the passenger seat watching the driver cast furtive glances in his rear-view mirror.

"Is she all right?" he asked tentatively.

"Yeah, she'll be fine..." Sophie tried to sound as sober as she could. "Just a... left, here please mate. Yes, near the church."

"We should go to that church, Soph," Sarah chimed in from the back.

"No we shouldn't, I'd only combust."

No sooner had they arrived home than Sarah opened a bottle of wine, while Helen spirited Keith upstairs. The slamming door wouldn't open again for sixteen hours, and he would emerge having pulled four muscles and put his back out.

Sophie found herself in the cold, sobering bathroom, though not sober enough to shake off the sleepy haze that had crept over her. She shuddered, anticipating the headache that awaited her in the morning. She she sat on the toilet, knees and ankles pressed together, her head swayed to the beat of eighties classics pumping from the living room downstairs.

Suddenly, Sarah stormed in, fire in her eyes. "Are you trying to make me look fucking stupid?" she barked, snatching the toilet roll from Sophie's hand.

"Eh?" Sophie responded ineloquently. "I'm only having a wee."

"Look at my face, there's lipstick everywhere. Are you trying to make a fool of me?"

"What? No!"

"Look at the state of my fucking face," Sarah repeated, furiously wiping traces of red lipstick from her mouth and cheek.

"I am not having an argument with you while my knickers are round my ankles. Give me a second." Sophie huffed and flushed.

Sarah hit the tap and a sharp stream of warm water bounced off the basin and splashed everything within a foot radius.

Sophie washed her hands as Sarah frantically scrubbed any trace of Sophie from her lips. She stopped. She stood still and stared at her reflection like a hunting lion who had come to pass the surface of a lake and paused for breath.

Sarah placed her palms firmly on the sides of the bowl and dropped her head to stare at the plug, her rage softened. "You don't understand…" she pleaded quietly, her voice beginning to break.

"Then tell me."

Sarah faced Sophie, who reached to wipe a spot of water from her chin. "You just don't… understand," she repeated. "I want you… I want you to be able to meet my friends. I don't want you to be a secret, it's not fair."

"Is that why you're upset?"

"Tell me, are you happy?" Sarah asked, her eyes glossy with tears.

"Yes. Promise," Sophie answered as Sarah wrapped her hands around her waist.

"I just love you so much…"

The steady silence was only marred by the sound of the cistern refilling.

Sophie awoke bleary-eyed the next day, with Sarah still face-down and snoring beside her. She felt as if she hadn't slept at all, partly due to the vodka and partly due to those three words that had infected her deepest sleep. They were uttered in a drunken haze where only one of them would remember they were ever said at 2 a.m. in the dark bathroom.

She pushed at the lock button of her phone. One p.m. She squinted thoughtfully; it made sense given they did not go to sleep until three in the morning.

01:57 – Tinder: You have received a new message from Darren

Who the fuck was Darren? Sophie blinked furiously into focus. This wasn't her phone.

Sophie dropped it onto the carpet like a hot pan handle, her hands fumbling in search of her own device as her brain ping-ponged between questions and her stomach tied itself in knots.

Had Sarah been messaging him? Recently? While they were together? Before she told Sophie she loved her? Did she message first, or was this unsolicited? If it was unsolicited, then surely Sarah had been actively swiping, and recently too. It was December; they got back together in September. That's three months. But then again, they had never explicitly said they were exclusive. Still, Sophie was sure they weren't dating other people. How could they, when they spent all their free time together?

Or did she not love Sophie at all? Was it a drunken slip of the tongue, something she would neither remember nor repeat?

She could be looking for somebody else. Sure, Sophie had seen the app on Sarah's phone before, with its annoying red notifications that would appear and disappear again. But those were from a time when they didn't love each other, and this was now. This was the morning after soft, tender kisses and public displays of affection, and those three little words that terrified her.

Insecurity charged towards her at full speed. Sophie stopped still and lay back into the duvet, forcing herself to ignore it.

"Jesus, Sophie. What are you going to do?" Kirsten asked with Lauren humming in agreement.

"I don't know." Sophie sighed and looked up from her seat, cross-legged on the carpet with her fingers dancing around the stem of her glass. "She was pretty plastered at the time, then she spent forty minutes insisting she wasn't gay, another forty minutes making me listen to Damien Rice and then ended the night by taking me upstairs by the scruff of my neck."

"Wahey, I bet you enjoyed that!" whooped Maria, throwing her head back and laughing loudly, her black curls bouncing with each delighted shake.

"Yes, and you'd know!" Lauren shot back quickly.

"But what if she is gay, though?" Kirsten suggested.

Chapter Fifteen

Charlie zoomed straight for Sarah's ankles on his new tricycle, bow still attached, as Caro yelled after him not to scratch the laminate floor – as if a toddler gave a toss about how much per square metre she'd paid for it.

Sarah dived aside, swiftly scooping him from the red, yellow, and blue plastic bike, planting a kiss on his cheek before setting him down. He pulled a face, wiping off the kiss, and dashed back to the Christmas tree to hunt for more treasures amid mountains of torn wrapping paper.

The house brimmed with the aroma of turkey and gravy. Excited shrieks echoed from Caro's youngest, nine-month-old Conan, babbling in his bouncing chair. Sarah felt a pang of longing, regretting living so far from home and coveting what Caroline had: the big house, lovely husband, and gorgeous little children.

It was her first visit home since 'The Greek Incident' – as they'd dubbed it – and they'd resolved not to mention it again. Well, that was the promise her mother had made after trying to broach the subject on Christmas Eve and being promptly shut down.

"Sarah!" came a hiss from the top of the stairs. She turned to see Fiona crouched at the top and gesturing to her through the white balustrades.

"Merry fucking Christmas to you too," Sarah grumbled as she was dragged to the upstairs bathroom.

Fiona's hair had escaped its chic bun, heavy curls now hanging around her collarbones. Her toothy smile belied the borderline hysterical tone of her voice and wide-eyed panic. She paced barefoot, snatching a blue gift box from atop the cistern.

"No, it's not a vibrator before you ask. I know I've done that before and you fell for it last time, but serious now. Serious face on."

Sarah peered into the box, then jerked her head up so quickly she nearly gave herself whiplash. "Pregnant? Seriously?"

"Ten tests seriously," Fiona confirmed solemnly, reclaiming the box.

"Oh my God, that's amazing. I'm so happy! Fi–" she paused, "what's wrong?"

The petite woman sat on the lid of the toilet with her cream jumper pulled up around her face, her strawberry blonde hair caught up in the hands covering her eyes.

"Mam's going to go mad."

"Ah, fer fuck's sake now, don't be daft. She'll be thrilled! Craig doesn't know yet, does he?"

"No, you're the only one I've told. He'll be all right though, won't he?"

"Yes, yes, he'll be fine! He'll make a great father, you know he will. Why are you scared of telling Mam?"

"I'm twenty-seven, I'm not married, what will everybody think?"

"You've been with Craig for five years, it's hardly like you've harpooned the first bloke you saw in The White Horse and got knocked up."

Sarah sat steadfast at the head of the long pine table, littered with the corpses of crackers and novelty festive paraphernalia. This Christmas mirrored every other: Finnoula opposite Fred, Caroline opposite Graham, Fiona opposite Craig, and she sat on the end, single.

That morning they were herded to Mass by her Mam who stood at the door shouting up the stairs like she was at the Last Post. They'd bid farewell to the priest, holding their breath as Finnoula invited him for tea – which she did every year – and they exhaled in relief as he declined, thankful to avoid conversing with a boring man with halitosis.

It took approximately three hours for their Mam to cremate the turkey so it would suck the saliva from their mouths. Sarah envied the baby who had his food blended.

Sarah observed her family in that moment of familial chaos. Finnoula in an intense discussion with Graham over the price of beef. Fiona and Craig gazed at each other, doe-eyed; Sarah had no doubt the news had been shared and well-received. She was genuinely thrilled for them. Caroline wiped puree from Conan's chin while Charlie rocketed around the hallway, bored with the adults. Her father focused solely on his plate, and faint smoke wafted from the kitchen.

Sarah, the eldest by at least four years, seemed to have little to show for it. Her mind conjured shapes and phantoms of good fortune past: Charlie's birth, Caroline's wedding, the moment they'd announced Conan's impending arrival with a blue birthday cake for her mother. When Sarah had imagined her future, she'd pictured exactly this – except the children would be her own, with a husband by her side.

Then came the guilt, looming like a spectre and nestling uncomfortably close. She was in a serious relationship with potential, but Sophie was forbidden territory; nobody would accept them. How could they? She was in her late thirties and in love with a woman ten years her junior.

Sophie would only end up hurt, again. How could Sarah entertain thoughts of a future knowing her reality would tear her family apart?

The shrill squeal of the fire alarm jolted Sarah from her daze.

"Ah, Mam's burnt the fucking pudding."

"Fuck! Fuck!" said Charlie, rocketing through the living room with his feet raised in the air. "Fuck! Fuck!"

"Jesus, Fiona, don't swear in front of the children."

"Jeeeeeeesus, Fiona," the toddler mimicked.

"Charlie, don't take the Lord's name in vain. That's very naughty," Finnoula shouted, dashing into the kitchen.

"Mam, that should be the last of your worries when you're on the brink of burning the fucking house down."

"Fiona!" Caroline yelled amidst the chaos as smoke billowed in from the kitchen. "Use a different word, like *baguette*."

"I'll be coming after you with a fuckin' baguette. We've no pudding – at Christmas! Can ye believe?" Fiona fumed. "I tell ye what, we won't be wrapping up our child in cotton wool like you do yours, will we now Craig?"

"Child?"

"Ah, Jesus..." Craig muttered, grimacing behind his hand.

"I'm sorry now, what child?" Finnoula poked her head back around the door. "Fred! Stop being a lummox and see to the pudding. Now, will somebody tell me what child?"

"I'm bleeding pregnant, aren't I?" Fiona said.

The alarm kept wailing, the smoke kept coming, the coughing started and then the piercing shriek stopped. Fred emerged wafting a tea towel and opening the doors and windows to let the crisp winter air run through the house.

Sarah stood on the periphery of the chaos and left without a word, grabbing a bottle of wine on her way out.

The wind whipped around them, tugging at their hair and clothes like an impatient child. Sarah and Aoife huddled closer on the weathered bench at Harty's Quay, its paint peeling away to reveal the greying wood beneath – not unlike the clouds above that had scrubbed away any hint of blue from the sky.

"Have ye ever had one of those health bars?" Aoife said, plonking down next to Sarah. "You know, the ones with no gluten, no sugar, no wheat an' no personality. I tell ye, it's one of the worst things I've ever put in my mouth, and I've had a lot of nasty shit in there."

Sarah looked to her left and laughed, grateful for the distraction.

"You know, my Mam shouted up the stairs fifteen minutes ago and said, 'Aoife, there's a nob walking down Rochestown Road looking like Dora the Explorer and it looks an awful lot like Sarah McCarthy.' And then I got your text and I thought, I bet when I get there she'll be staring out to the sea like a feckin' war widow."

"Did she? Did your Mam really say that?"

"No, you dozy bollocks. She did see you though when she drove past from my Uncle Steve's. Give me that bottle here–" Aoife picked up the green bottle and uncorked it with her keys. "You've not even opened it! There's no point in a bottle of wine if it's not open."

Sarah took the bottle from Aoife and took a sip. "Thanks for coming to see me. Merry Christmas, you big bitch. How's it going?"

"I'm still texting that fella I met at our Christmas drinks in Dub. He's nice." Aoife paused thoughtfully. "Massive cock."

"It's chaos at home. Mam burnt the pudding, Charlie's going off swearing, and Fiona's pregnant."

"Oh, that's lovely! I tell you though, doesn't it make you feel like you're left behind? Everybody going off, getting married and having kids and do you know what I'm going through? Puberty. Look at me, I've got feckin' spots everywhere."

"Ah, you're a tonic. Stop hogging that wine though."

"Sure they'll notice you've gone."

"Eventually, yeah. And then they'll call me, but hopefully I can have a bit of peace before then."

The bench was wet when she sat but she'd warmed to the cold wood. Sarah's mind drifted to Sophie, remembering their Saturday on the sofa watching box sets, the younger woman drifting in and out of sleep. Pale skin wrapped up in her dressing gown, the one Caroline bought her last Christmas, pink lips pursed, the rhythmic rise and fall of her chest. Sarah had paused the TV just to watch her, the silence softly broken by tender breath.

For weeks on end, they would not spend a day apart. Mornings began together, snoring stopped with a gentle kiss on the back of the neck as Sarah came out of her slumber to turn over and bury herself in Sophie's arms, begging to snooze for five more minutes which would turn into ten or fifteen.

As the sea before them churned restlessly, white-capped waves crashing against the shore, Sarah found herself caught between the comfort of Aoife's familiar banter and the secret warmth of her thoughts of Sophie.

The tide of guilt swelled and tears pricked the back of her eyes. She had to tell somebody, she had to.

"Are you all right, Saz?" Aoife asked.

Sarah shook her head fervently. "No. No I'm not."

Aoife wrapped her arm around her shoulders. "Is it work?"

Sarah shook her head, the tears coming down her cheeks and sadness holding her throat.

"Family?"

Sarah shook her head again and sniffed.

"Here, have some wine." Aoife wrapped Sarah's fingers around the neck of the bottle and raised it encouragingly.

There was an iron weight pressing down on her chest and expelling the air from her lungs. She dragged in a deep breath of cold air to calm her thundering heart.

Silence.

'I'm in love with a woman,' she wanted to say, but couldn't. Every word after 'I' stalled on the tip of her tongue.

"Here, I'll tell you something I learnt which would cheer you up," Aoife said, and Sarah breathed a sigh of relief. "Do you remember a girl from school called Katherine O'Connor? She was a shy, mousy thing. I think we were in the same maths class."

Sarah nodded.

"Well, she's just announced she's a massive lesbian. Everybody is absolutely flabbergasted. I can't get over it. That's like *you* telling me you're a lesbian."

Oh my God, Sarah thought, and the tears started again.

At some point in the distant future, Sarah would look back on that moment and realise how tragically ironic it was. She'd be at the kitchen sink and staring out of the window to a time where her life was very different, and she'd smile to herself before small hands tugged at the hem of her skirt for a biscuit.

"Ah, come on now Saz. Whatever it is, can't be that bad. I know work has been really having an effect on you lately, but you just can't take everything to heart..."

She never got her words out. Aoife didn't make her, knowing that whatever it was, Sarah would tell her when she was ready. And that night when Sarah went to bed with the warm glow of alcohol to comfort her, she texted Sophie.

Sarah – 00:02: I miss you x

Sophie – 00:03: I miss you too x

Chapter Sixteen

"Kevin, don't you dare touch that before dinner," Sophie said as the form of her father the glutton hovered over her rosemary roasted potatoes. *Slap.* Right over the back of his hand. He tittered and scurried away out of the kitchen.

"Is he causing trouble again, duckie?" Little Mammy popped her head around the door. "Kevin, pack it in, you useless sod."

"I just wanted to check it was all right!" Kevin shouted in response from the lounge. Sophie heard him cheers her brother as if they were in cahoots together.

Sophie adored Christmas. It was the build-up of excitement as party invites landed in her inbox and the Christmas lights hovered over Oxford Circus and everybody clambered off to the pub in festive spirits at any opportunity. For a short while, everybody, even Hector, seemed to cheer up.

Every Christmas, Sophie would stand at the end of the driveway of their terraced house, knowing that on the other side of the door, lying in wait, was Kevin in an apron making a tiramisu. Little Mammy would be counting the bottles of Baileys he had stashed under the stairs and telling him he'd bought too many (never too many for Christmas).

Her brother Luke, armed with a highlighter and the TV guide her parents insisted on buying, would be planning their Christmas viewing for the week. There would be at least half a day where she would hide upstairs and pretend not to be home to avoid certain members of her extended family.

The big day started the same each year. Kevin would bound upstairs with the enthusiasm of a Labrador on steroids, announce he'd make breakfast and insist that everybody came downstairs. He would be stood, at sixty-two years old, next to the kitchen table where he'd lined up four flutes of Buck's fizz and grinning as proud as punch.

Little Mammy rolled her eyes and let Kevin drink hers like he knew she would, which is why he made four when only three people were interested. Though he was twenty-five, Luke was always the first one sat beside the tree. He sat cross-legged on the wooden floor while she, her Mum and Kevin sat on the sofas.

Sophie knew exactly what lurked behind the wrapping paper because every year she wrote a list. Not just any list, mind you, but a detailed one with links to items, sizes, and preferred colours. Wasting money was sacrilege, and Sophie had strict terms: *don't deviate from the list*, lest she end up with another build-your-own ukulele kit, courtesy of Luke's misguided creativity.

Luke, equally anal-retentive, also knew his presents in advance. His gifts were like him – serious and practical – while Sophie's revolved around food, wine, or homeware. She welcomed pots and pans; Luke preferred hefty tomes on astrophysics and other yawn-inducing subjects.

Their common ground? A dry sense of humour, a love of cocktails, and the fact they were both raging homosexuals. When Sophie realised she was gay in their little Catholic school, she thought if anyone told Luke, he'd be bullied mercilessly. It never crossed her mind he might be gay too.

Their coming out was accidental. Luke invited Sophie to dinner after school, promising her favourite dessert. She should've known something was up – he was being suspiciously nice. But free dinner and a chocolate fudge cake? She wasn't about to question her fifteen-year-old brother's sudden generosity.

And then, just after she had finished her cake, he placed his elbows on the table and leaned in. "Sophie, I've got something to tell you."

At that moment Sophie thought, 'fuck, I know what's coming,' and everything fell into place. How Luke had spent more time than usual in his room, being secretive, chatting to people on the internet and not disclosing who or why. They used to be close and now he was acting differently, but she was too busy studying or working to notice.

She'd whispered those same words down the phone to a friend three years prior.

Sophie held her breath, hoping she'd jumped to the wrong conclusion. It wasn't self-hatred, but fear of others' reactions to her shy, sensitive brother. He couldn't hold his partner's hand in Manchester without provoking some thug in cheap jeans and a knock-off T-shirt.

"Sophie, I'm gay."

"Oh, that's alright, because I am too," she blurted, draining her drink. Luke sat, gobsmacked. In hindsight, it made sense – she'd never had a proper boyfriend and had a particular fondness for Charlize Theron.

She flagged down the waiter. "Excuse me, I'm going to need another drink, please."

By the grace of a God she didn't believe in, Luke stuck to the list and bought her a beautiful emerald clutch bag wrapped in velvet with a gold clasp at the front. Sophie stroked the fabric one way and then the other, watching as it changed colour as she drew lines as if she were a child drawing with her fingertip on Grandma's pink sofa.

"Is that a bag?" Kevin asked and moved closer. "Doesn't it have a strap on?"

"No, Dad. I think she's already got one of those!" Luke fired back. Little Mammy choked on her tea. Sophie stared wide-eyed at the two cackling men.

"Kevin!" Little Mammy chastised.

"It wasn't me, it was Luke!"

Sophie imagined Sarah by her side, nestled in the warmth of her clan experiencing the chaotic joy of a family that accepted love in all its forms. She wondered how Sarah might feel if she could witness firsthand the aftermath of coming out, the acceptance that followed the initial shock.

If she tasted, even just for a second, what it felt like to live unapologetically, it might bolster her confidence and encourage tentative steps towards a future they wanted but couldn't speak of.

The thought brought a bittersweet smile to Sophie's lips. Yet Sophie knew that unless she was certain that day would come, she couldn't fully invest herself in their relationship. The risk of heartbreak loomed too large to let go completely.

Chapter Seventeen

Thunder ripped and rumbled in the belly of blue clouds that had been gathering for days. Lightning flashed over figures on pavements, their coats pulled over heads as they darted between deep puddles and doorways.

Sophie, Lauren, and Craig had decided to spend New Year's Eve at Sophie's flat. They considered it a grown-up decision. 'January's long enough without going to a shit bar and pissing my money away on New Year's Eve to make the month longer,' Craig had said, and they agreed he made an excellent point.

Lauren arrived carrying half a crate of champagne. If they were staying in, they'd still get as drunk as if they'd gone out. 'And we get to choose the music,' Lauren reminded her – another selling point. It also reminded Sophie to exile the coffee table to the kitchen; she could do without Craig crashing into it and breaking his arm like last time they had a flat party.

Party? Could three people constitute a party? A small gathering, perhaps. But it was New Year's Eve – it needed a sense of occasion rather than feeling like an ordinary skint Saturday before payday.

"That pasta smells good, Soph," Lauren said as she heaved the sodden box onto the table. It was a small miracle the bottom hadn't given way, littering the pavement with puddles of fizz and glass.

"Here she is!" Craig sauntered into the kitchen, dressed head to toe in hot pink.

"You've been working out. Look at that arse," said Lauren. He turned around for her to slap it.

"You know, I was in Selfridges today and I was doing a little shopping in Elizabeth Arden to look for something to give my face a little pep. Look at the creases around my eyes." Lauren stepped closer and thrust her face into Sophie's and then into Craig's so they could see the lines which appeared like valleys to Lauren, and faint age-appropriate creases to everybody else.

"Anyway," she continued. "The woman there was telling me about these new capsules with hyaluronic acid which I deposit once a day. And I looked at her and said, 'Up my bum, yeah?' and she looked at me like I'd grown another head. She said 'No, you break them over your face!' and I've spent all day wondering how far I had bought into the beauty industry that I wouldn't question putting things up my arse."

"Oh my God, I had no idea where that story was going for a second," Craig cackled as Sophie launched her head back with laughter. "Here, get one of those bottles open," said Craig.

Three bottles later and it was close to midnight. She sat next to Lauren on the brown leather sofa which sagged in the middle. She could feel the heavy wooden frame jab her buttocks. Messages from Sarah had been sparse over the last ten days – a snatched phone call here and there – and she wondered whether the Irishwoman thought about her at all when they were apart.

The Tinder notification worried her. In fact, it more than worried her. But what right really did she have to be so unnerved about it? They had never discussed any form of exclusivity or official relationship. Technically speaking, Sarah could do whatever she liked with whomever.

Maybe she should do the same. For a second she drunkenly considered downloading Tinder too, but the second really was fleeting because she soon decided she couldn't be bothered. Anybody on a dating app on New Year's Eve wasn't worth the time it took to talk to them.

Sophie felt as if she was walking on a bridge at the risk of collapsing, afraid of setting one foot wrong which would see everything crumble under her. Then she supposed there could be logic behind expecting a collapse, but how surprised could she be if and when it came? But also, if she expected it to end, then would she not be giving them a chance, knowing that it was all too futile?

Sophie found herself raking over conversations and snippets of words that irked her. Words uttered under the influence and in the dead of night with only each other for company. Words that were never usually remembered the next day, or were but went unacknowledged.

"If you were a man, you'd be perfect for me."

"Well fuck you, I'm not a man and I never will be," Sophie had responded.

Well, she hadn't. She should have done but she didn't want the bridge to collapse. So when Sarah said those three little words in the dimly-lit en-suite before Christmas, only weeks later, the cutting comments were put aside. What did they matter when love usurped all?

Though Sarah had made no mention of the L-word in their brief communications since, and Sophie half expected to never hear it again.

She understood – coming out wasn't easy. It was to be expected that Sarah had the same insecurities simmering away inside that she had once had herself. For the time being, their secrecy was a necessary burden to bear until Sarah was ready, if she'd ever be ready. Sophie was not so unreasonable that she had forgotten how difficult a journey it was.

"When do I get to meet Sarah?" Lauren asked, as if reading her mind.

Sophie shifted uncomfortably. "I'm not sure, Lauren. It's... complicated."

Lauren leaned forward. "How often do you see her?"

"Oh, you know, once a week or so," Sophie lied, avoiding eye contact.

Craig snorted from his armchair. "Once a week? Come off it, Soph. You two practically live together."

Sophie shot him a glare as Lauren's eyebrows shot up.

"Practically living together? Sophie, are you in love with her?"

Sophie's silence was answer enough.

"Sophie. This is, without doubt, the worst idea since I thought anti-bacterial shower gel could stop you getting pregnant."

"Hold on a second..." started Craig.

"Lauren, you cannot put Sanex up your hoo-ha like it's a spermicide!"

"I know that *now,*" Lauren scowled.

Lauren's mind raced with worry, a knot forming in her stomach. She berated herself silently. She should've stepped in when Sophie first mentioned meeting Sarah. If she had, she might've nipped this whole mess in the bud, sparing Sophie some heartbreak and herself a splitting headache.

Try as she might, Lauren couldn't envision a scenario where Sophie's heart wouldn't end up shattered again. It was like watching a car crash in slow motion, and she felt powerless to stop it.

Sure, she hadn't been around for the opening act of the Sarah Saga, but she'd heard enough retrospective tales to piece together the plot. And from where she was sitting, this sequel looked set to be even more of an emotional rollercoaster than the original.

Lauren took a long swig of her drink, wishing it could wash away the foreboding feeling settling in her chest. She was going to be front and centre for whatever came next, ready to pick up the pieces if – or, more likely, when – it all went tits up.

Sophie was grateful for her friend's concern but unsure how to reconcile it with her feelings for Sarah.

The topic of meeting friends was a minefield. Sarah visibly tensed when it was even hinted at. There was always a reason, always an excuse, but in time she would come out of that and hopefully Lauren would see that there was nothing malicious about Sarah at all. She was just a woman who was scared of her feelings.

"Well, while we're on the topic of confessions," Lauren said, bolstered by the booze enough to change the conversation, "I'm quitting my job on Monday."

Sarah drummed her fingers impatiently on the handle of her suitcase. The departure gates of Dublin Airport bustled with post-holiday travellers, but Sarah's mind was already in London. Three nights with friends in Dublin over New Year's had been lovely, truly, but she was itching to return to her life in the city. To Sophie.

The thought of Sophie sent a familiar warmth through her, quickly followed by a pang of guilt. She'd invited Sarah to spend New Year's Eve at her flat, and for a wild moment, Sarah had considered cancelling her Dublin plans. But reality had quickly reasserted itself. It wouldn't have been just the two of them, would it? Craig would've been there – fine enough, he was to Sophie what Helen was to Sarah. But Lauren... meeting Lauren was a hurdle Sarah wasn't quite ready to clear.

It wasn't that Sophie hadn't tried. She'd hinted at it numerous times, each suggestion met with telling silence. Sophie never pushed, which Sarah appreciated. And yet... sometimes, a small part of Sarah wished she would push, just a little. The imbalance of it all – Sarah calling the shots, Sophie acquiescing – made her feel uneasy.

The truth was, Sarah wasn't entirely opposed to meeting Sophie's friends. Not really. But the prospect terrified her. What did they know? What didn't they know? Did they see her as some heartless bitch, toying with their friend's emotions? Would they be polite to her face but whisper judgements behind her back? Or worse, would they confront her directly, laying bare their disapproval?

It was easier to say nothing, to exist in a perpetual state of 'maybe later' rather than committing to a 'yes' or 'no'.

Sarah's phone buzzed, and her heart leapt. Sophie? But no, it was Tinder again. *Ryan.* She felt guilty.

She never should have downloaded the bloody thing. But her friends had been relentless, insisting she needed to 'get over Chris by getting under some other fella'. If only they knew. So she'd played along, swiping half-heartedly, each match feeling like a betrayal.

Ryan had seemed nice enough. Handsome, with broad shoulders and a well-groomed beard. 'Are we sure he's Irish with a tan like that?' Aoife had joked. Sarah had responded to his first message with a perfunctory, 'I'm well thanks, you?' and then… nothing. She should have deleted the app months ago, but keeping it felt like part of the charade. Single Sarah, living it up in London, not Sarah-hopelessly-in-love-with-Sophie.

As she stared at the notification, Sarah felt the weight of her deception pressing down on her. She was hurting Sophie, even if Sophie had no idea. Not knowingly, perhaps, but hurting her all the same. And for what? To maintain a facade for friends who might very well accept her if she just gave them the chance?

The final boarding call for her flight crackled over the PA system. Sarah took a deep breath, squared her shoulders, and made her way to the gate. It was time to go home. To Sophie. And maybe, just maybe, it was time to start being brave.

Chapter Eighteen

"I've missed this," Sarah purred as she crawled into bed beside Sophie and wrapped herself around her. "I'm going to say something and it's not because I've had a glass of wine, I promise."

Sophie instinctively tensed.

"I love you, Like, I really love you."

Sophie smiled down at the woman who had moved her chin to rest on her chest to watch her face react. "I love you too," she responded, and Sarah showered her bare neck with kisses before planting one on her lips.

It felt nice – wonderful, actually, Sophie thought. For the first time the bridge felt stronger than it was when she first stepped on it. Those three words were the support for her to be bolder, for them to be more open and free, because who throws love away so easily regardless of how it came to be?

"I've never been this happy," Sarah whispered to the darkness before she fell asleep.

A semblance of a future that might exist for them after all blossomed like a determined flower peeking out from the crack of a flagstone. In spite of the secret which loomed over them, where nobody in Sarah's life knew she existed, Sophie allowed her mind to wander to places her low expectations had previously forbidden her from.

Sophie watched the sleeping woman on her chest, her features lit up by the moonlight that crept in through a gap in the blinds. She imagined what their future could look like.

Sarah wanted children. Sophie had never thought herself to be the mothering type, but she could come around to that idea. She would make a decent Mum, actually, she thought.

During the number of times Sophie had heard the 'when you find the right person' trope brought out when she turned her nose up at reproducing, she laughed and changed the topic. But now she feared the naysayers had been right after all. What a strange turn of events it was that she found the woman she was looking for in the most unexpected of places, as if she had been created just for her.

Sophie was on the cusp of dangerous territory in building a theoretical world she had no idea she would ever live in. This fantasy she had created was so distant yet, for the first time, had started to feel possible. If the woman professed to love Sophie as she did, then panic could not deter them. People searched for years to find what they had discovered quite by accident.

At some point between naming their children and deciding on the colour of their living room, Sophie fell into a dreamless slumber.

January was a funny month, Sophie thought, as she sat on the Overground to Islington and watched the city pass by in a blur of tower blocks and terraces. The gaiety and garishness of Christmas so quickly faded into nothing, as if it had never happened at all. One day, the streets were a riot of twinkling lights and festive cheer, shop windows brimming with tinsel and baubles, and the next, it was as if someone had flipped a switch, plunging London into a grey, post-holiday malaise.

The bare branches of trees that had once been adorned with fairy lights now stood stark against the slate-coloured sky, their silhouettes a reminder of the long winter ahead. Even the faces of her fellow passengers seemed to reflect this abrupt transition, their expressions a mix of resigned weariness and fading holiday cheer, as if they were all collectively nursing an emotional hangover from the season's excesses.

Sophie found herself oddly fascinated by this annual metamorphosis, how a city could transform so completely in the span of a few short days, shedding its festive skin to reveal the raw, unadorned reality beneath.

Winter seemed so much longer when the promise of presents and overindulgence was removed from the equation and sunshine and spring seemed so far away. What Sophie did enjoy about that time of the year, and she would stress that it was the only thing that she enjoyed, was that the misery bound everybody together in a Blitz-like spirit. The only topic of conversation ever seemed to be how poor they were (she was), how payday seemed so far away (also true, she was on day eighty-four of January) and how they couldn't wait for spring.

"Why is it that when people are doing cocaine, they always end up doing it in the kitchen?" Kirsten said, taking a swig of her beer and gesturing at the TV.

"Probably because it's harder to get out of upholstery." Sophie suggested.

"Sophie, why has your Dad sent me a photo of a cactus with the caption 'big prick'?" asked Lauren.

"He's adopted you as a daughter. Just go with it," Sophie laughed. The snap of a shutter caught her off-guard as she finished the last of the cava in her glass. "What was that for?"

"I've sent him a photo of you with the message 'bigger prick'," she chortled.

"To Sophie's Dad?" Kirsten interjected.

"Okay, we're out of wine," Sophie announced, swiftly redirecting the course of the conversation to the most pressing issue at hand. "It's eleven o'clock – the shops are closed, what are we going to do?"

"There's an off-licence down the road open twenty-four hours, come on," Maria said as she stood to put on her coat. "Babe? Will you look after Lauren and make sure she doesn't get herself into trouble please?"

"Aye, Captain!" Kirsten saluted and laughed.

The night was bitingly cold, a stark reminder of January's unforgiving nature. Maria and Sophie huddled close as they trudged along the pavement, their breath forming small clouds that dissipated quickly in the frigid air. Maria linked her arm through Sophie's to steady them against any slips on dark patches of ice, knowing that if one fell, the other would topple too.

The off-licence glowed like a beacon in the distance, its fluorescent lights cutting through the gloom. The promise of shelter, however temporary, spurred them on. The wind seemed determined to impede their progress, pushing against them with invisible hands, as if nature itself disapproved of their late-night booze run.

Empty crisp packets skittered across the pavement and branches thrashed mercilessly. With relief they finally reached the off-licence's door, the cheerful jingle of the bell as they entered a stark contrast to the tempest they'd just escaped. As the door swung shut behind them, Sophie took the opportunity to check her phone as Maria disappeared to the beer fridge.

23:14 – Sarah: I really miss you. What time will you be home? Xx

23:15 – Sophie: An hour or two yet, my love.

23:15 – Sarah: Good xx

"So, did she not want to come tonight then, Sarah?" Maria asked, returning with three bottles of Pinot Noir.

"I think she's too scared you'll all judge her," said Sophie.

The Spaniard paused. "We just want you to be happy, Soph. Find a nice lesbian to settle down with, cottage in the country, matching undercuts..."

Sophie snorted.

"Seriously, Sophie," Maria chided. "It's not fair on you. How long has it been now? We're at the end of January so... five months? And she's shown no desire to meet your friends."

Sophie fiddled with the chocolate bars on the front of the counter, lining them up neatly.

"You're a nice person. You answer the door even when you know Jehovah's Witnesses are on the other side," Maria said softly. "I'm just worried it's not going to end well."

Chapter Nineteen

"Hi Mam, are you OK?"

Fiona had taken a photo of her Mam's face when she found out the Christmas pudding was on fire and had sent it to the group chat. It had consequently become Finnoula's contact picture and made Sarah smile whenever she rang.

"Yes, I'm good thank you. How are ye doing? Are you in the car? You sound like you're far away."

"Yes, Mam. I don't know if I've managed to get the speaker working properly. Can you still hear me?"

"Aye. I won't be long, I was just calling to tell you that I've found a nice man for you. Doreen – you know, next door – has a sister Margaret who has a nephew who lives in Dublin. He's single, good job, nice-looking from the photo I saw, and I've passed on your number for him. I hope you don't mind…"

Sarah sighed.

Her Mam had taken one look at her at Christmas and decided it was high time that Sarah got back on the dating wagon. She had since enlisted her network of friends who reached the length and breadth of Ireland and were all seemingly on a search to find her a new man.

In the past week alone she had fielded calls from a nervous-sounding man, Peter, from Waterford who owned a chemist, Neil from Ballyshannon who ran a builders' yard and Michael from Castlebar who made leather pig masks for an international fetish group.

"Mam, I'm just going to stop you there. Will you please stop pimping me out to everyone you meet?"

"I'm not, I'm just trying to help." Sarah pictured her mother, perched on the hallway bench with the landline cradled in the crook of her neck. Her knees pressed together because 'ladies don't cross their legs', and her ankles tucked underneath her, 'you know, in the way Kate Middleton does'. For a moment, Sarah felt for every man in Cork without a ring on his finger who had been approached by her mental mother, throwing around photos of Sarah like confetti.

"No, you're meddling. Will you stop?"

"You don't have time on your side, Sarah, I thought that's why you were going to settle down with Chris..."

Sarah put her foot down and took the slip road off the motorway. She yawned. The four o'clock alarm that morning hadn't been kind to her; she was thankful Sophie was still asleep when she left so she didn't see what a fright Sarah looked in the light of day.

"Mam, I don't have the time for this. Look, I have a work call coming in. I'll speak to you later," Sarah lied.

The car beneath her hummed and jolted with every slight dip in the tarmac; her beloved black BMW Coupé had been temporarily replaced with a ten-year-old Citroën and the contrast was stark. It made the drive up to Newcastle more arduous than it needed to be.

She wondered how long it would be until Finnoula suggested that she 'looked abroad' and posted her a brochure for Egypt; 'they take anybody, you know'. Sarah shuddered at the thought of her mother trying to sell her for two camels and six sheep. Maybe she'd turn the tables, sell Finnoula, settle for one camel and buy herself a life of peace and quiet.

The mid-winter sun was rising in a bright blue sky, casting shadows of pylons on bare fields. Such a sun could persuade a person that it wasn't completely Baltic outside when, in fact, the temperature would rob you of breath.

The new year hadn't been kind to her. Work pressure mounted and she spent far too many late nights at her computer while Sophie slept upstairs, having banned the laptop from bed. *Cheeky mare*, Sarah thought, it was her bed, but she loved that Sophie spent most nights in it.

She wouldn't have conceded had she not thought Sophie had a point; the only machine her girlfriend would accept as the third person in their relationship couldn't send emails and certainly didn't have a keyboard.

To ease the mounting pressure at work and give them something to look forward to before spring came, they'd booked a weekend away the month following. Sarah had been baffled at how Sophie had persuaded her to go to Budapest when she had argued vehemently for Venice, but anywhere with Sophie was good enough for her.

Even if it meant lying to her family about going to a conference about steel fabrication.

Admittedly she felt like she had stalled in her progress, or desire, to move their relationship forward. In the nights Sophie spent in her own bed and Sarah was alone, her doubts felt overwhelming. She was embarrassed she'd allowed herself to get carried away enough to suggest moving in together. They could have pretended they were housemates when her friends or family came to visit, but she suspected that was a step too far for Sophie so it remained unsaid.

Their getaway was a chance to fix that though. A chance to banish those doubts in her mind by revelling in the company of her love for three uninterrupted days away from prying eyes, and and remind herself that she and Sophie could have a future together.

It would be just her look though to bump into somebody from home, but she tried not to dwell on that thought for too long.

Before she knew it, she saw three towering cranes on the horizon and Sarah's stomach churned. Two of her Project Managers had abruptly quit, leaving the South Shields building site in disarray. She blamed herself for not paying more attention, but Sophie's words echoed: "You shouldn't need to micromanage two grown men doing the job they've been doing for fifteen years." Sarah cursed them both: at five a.m. when her alarm dragged her downstairs to work on emails, at seven a.m. during her drive to the far end of the country, and at eleven a.m. when she arrived on-site to face a raging architect.

A high-visibility jacket and hard hat awaited her arrival. Leather loafers crunching on sandy gravel, she marched silently with the architect to the project office, determined to assess the budget overrun and praying she'd still have a job afterwards.

Protected from the chill of the night by heat lamps positioned overhead and thick woollen coats, Sophie and Sarah sat at a wrought-iron table watching the light fade quickly. Joggers with taut stomachs on show, unperturbed by the mid-winter cold, passed by in twos.

A solitary tea light flickered defiantly in the wind and cast an unsteady glow over Sarah. The two women sat ensconced in a comfortable silence, the last plumes of smoke rising into the air from the ashtray interrupting their game of coy glances and grins. Then, as if a shadow had passed her grave, the frivolity drained from Sarah's face and she tilted her chin forward in the way she did when she had something serious to say. It was the look she gave Sophie as she considered what to say, determined to add weight to her words so they were not forgotten.

"Sophie, we're in a serious, long-term relationship..." she began, letting the sentence hang. Sarah watched Sophie straighten up, her lip pursing slightly as if bracing for bad news. *Don't worry, I'm not ending things,* Sarah thought, though it stung to see Sophie so readily expect hurt. "What is it that you see in me?"

"What sort of question is that?" Sophie stubbed her own cigarette on top of Sarah's.

"No, I'm being serious." Sarah's eyebrows furrowed in concentration and a deep vertical crease appeared with the intensity of her stare. "What I'm doing to you isn't fair... I wish you would just hit me sometimes, scream at me, just be angry for it."

"Then don't do it?" she responded simply, knowing the situation was far more complex. Sarah shifted uncomfortably in her seat. "Look, how can I be angry with you when I know what it is you're going through?"

"But you shouldn't be putting up with this because–"

Sophie cut her off. "The reasons you're about to list are all in your own head," she said firmly, "The fact of the matter is, I don't hate you. Not at all."

A cold hand reached out over the table in search of its partner. "Look at me," the Irishwoman whispered for her ears only. "I love you. I really do, and I've never been this happy."

Happiness for Sarah was the tender morning kisses that sent tingles down her spine, gently rousing her from sleep. It was waking next to Sophie's soft, warm body and feeling her arms snake around her waist in the morning.

But when she looked past the rosy hue of romance and into their reality, guilt surged like a wave, threatening to drag her under every time she lied to her mum, her sister, her friends, about what she was doing and with whom. How wrong it felt for a love like this to be confined to shadows and secrets.

Sophie was enough – more than enough. Funny, bright, warm, and perfect for Sarah, despite her occasional struggles with emotional articulation. But she was a woman, and that fact complicated everything.

Sarah could vividly imagine her mother's reaction: the colour draining from her face, her perfectly pink lips parted in shock, wordlessly uncrossing her ankles and leaving the room. Her father would sit alone on the sofa, Finnoula having shaken off his hand, his warm eyes downcast with his head in his hands, questioning where he went wrong. And Sarah would face their disappointment, wishing the ground would swallow her whole, shame creeping around her wrists like rope snakes carving valleys in her flesh.

Perhaps she should swap Sophie for Steven, to get them used to the idea that she was dating. Finnoula would sigh with relief and perhaps even stop putting out Lonely Heart adverts in the Post Office. It would end the secrecy, the lies to friends about her plans. Perhaps when everyone saw her happiness, they might look past the fact that it was with a woman rather than a man. Eventually.

Then she thought of the way Sophie braced herself for the worst thing Sarah could say without a word leaving her lips. Was she so convinced she would be hurt that she expected it quickly and without prior warning? Sarah hated it. She wanted Sophie to trust her, but what could she do?

Craig bought Fiona a ring after she announced their pregnancy and by New Year's Eve, the two were engaged. Fi was four months gone now and showed the sparkler off to anybody she hadn't bored to tears yet.

Perhaps she should make a statement of intent to prove she saw longevity in their relationship and demonstrated that she wanted it to work. It would give Sophie a reason to believe in them, to believe in her.

"Sophie, I want to ask you something," Sarah said, stubbing her cigarette out. She looked up at her girlfriend, eyes beginning to glaze over with equal parts tiredness and wine as she came to take Sophie's hands in her own.

"Mhmm?" Sophie hummed encouragingly.

"Will you move in with me?"

"No," Sophie replied too quickly, then scrambled to soften the blow. "I would love to, Sarah. But think about it, my love, how could I possibly?"

"Helen wouldn't mind, she adores you..." Sarah whispered, ashamed.

Sophie felt awful for shooting her down so hastily and extinguishing a flame she had so wanted to nurture. "But nobody knows I exist. When your friends or sister or parents come to stay – where will I go?"

Surely if her head was there, Sophie thought, *then there was a sign that there was a genuine future for the two of them. Surely...*

Yes, she should have handled the situation more delicately rather than reducing it to the sum of a knee-jerk reaction, but she knew her instinct was right.

"I would love to wake up beside you every morning, Sarah, but it's not fair to ask me to live lying to your friends and family about who I am to you when I would technically be in my own home." Sarah had gone quiet. "What would we say? We'd be backed into a corner and it's not right."

Sarah nodded slowly.

"When we're ready, when the time is right, we'll move in together," Sophie said into the growing silence. Sarah lit another cigarette.

Sophie remained optimistic yet cautiously cynical, knowing Sarah might not remember this conversation come morning.

Chapter Twenty

Daffodils beamed at Sophie from every available flowerbed; a clear sign that winter was retreating, and good riddance too. Barren trees sprouted bright green leaves with bluebells beginning to blossom at their roots.

April beckoned without much encouragement. The nights that Sarah spent at Sophie's flat became comfortably common. She and Craig had bonded after learning that his parents lived in Cork before moving to Kinsale, and after much discussion it appeared that Sarah knew their next-door neighbour.

'Everyone in Ireland knows each other, or of each other,' Sarah had said.

Nonsense, Sophie thought, until one March evening where Helen had brought a man home who had Irish family. It turned out he went to school with one of her thirty cousins, prompting Sarah to put two feet of distance between them – as if he hadn't just walked in on them kissing.

Meanwhile Boozy Lauren's departure loomed. The vein in Hector's temple became bigger and bluer until it was the only thing Sophie could concentrate on whenever he spoke. Lauren was the only Operations Director who'd ever stood up to his tantrums, and he'd begrudgingly accepted her leaving by pretending she had already left.

On Lauren's last day, the final hour dragged. At four p.m., she stood to applause and marched into Hector's office with her laptop and work phone, like a participant in the Changing of the Guard, and left the office for the pub. At six p.m., Sophie sent the final Spitalfields site marketing plans to the Senior Management Team and dashed out, only to find Oxford Circus Tube station mobbed so she ran to Bond Street instead.

It had been a remarkably dry start to the month but what the city lacked in rain it made up for in wind. A large gust rallied down Oxford Street, turning umbrellas inside out and blowing Sophie's wrap skirt apart, giving a group of middle-aged men an eyeful of her lace briefs.

That's their day made, she thought.

Lauren had chosen a bar very typical of East London, though why she had no idea. 'But we always go to Soho,' Sophie pointed out. 'Yes, exactly,' Lauren replied, 'and it's alright when I'm with you but I don't fancy being mistaken for being a lesbian in front of my colleagues.'

"I'm going to the bar!" Sophie shouted over the noise.

"Good idea – happy hour ends at seven. Stock up!" Lauren said, gesturing to the table of drinks before her.

Darren from Finance waded through the crowd with his tie strapped to his forehead, carrying a tray of shots above his head.

"Two of the Cosmos please," she said to the shaven-headed student in a striped shirt behind the bar.

She tapped her card on the machine as two pale purple martini glasses were slid in her direction. Sophie took them by the stems and squeezed herself between the crowds; she was just in time to see Lauren lean over a nearby table and promptly vomit all over it.

Dumbstruck onlookers watched on wide-eyed as the blue-brown liquid dripped onto the floor, Lauren's eyes half-glazed yet wide open in horror. Darren had jolted into some semblance of sobriety to pluck his bags swiftly from the banquettes in the vicinity before they became tainted by regurgitated sambuca.

She would have put her head in her hands, had she not been holding a cocktail in each one.

"Excuse me, Mr. Accounts Payable," Sophie called over to him. "Don't you scarper when we both know you've been the one feeding her shots all afternoon. Grab her things and follow me."

Downing a cocktail in one, Sophie took Lauren's arm with her newly free hand and yanked her towards the bathroom.

"Do I have to wait outside the ladies lavs?" Darren shouted through the cobalt-blue door. "This is embarrassing."

"Not as embarrassed as she'll be tomorrow morning when she wakes up and remembers what a tit of herself she made. How much did she drink anyway?" Sophie shouted back with a handful of Lauren's hair in one hand and her phone in the other as Lauren vomited again into the toilet.

"Thrhnnnr shots..." she could hear Darren mumble.

"Clearer please," she instructed.

"Might have been, like... nine drinks? A few of them were shots." Sophie winced. Lauren had only been gone two and a half hours. No wonder she was four sheets to the wind and her knees were threatening to go on strike.

"Fucking hell, Darren." She shouted back towards the door and waited as he heard him talk to somebody who she assumed to be staff. "That's it, Lauren, here have some water."

After another glass of water, a false alarm for vomiting again and a stern talking-to, Lauren emerged red-faced from the bathrooms and was escorted off the premises by security in a manner befitting her reputation.

Accompanied by her flatmate, Lauren was ferried home in a taxi leaving Sophie to meander through Spitalfields towards Liverpool Street without any further obligations for her evening. It would make a five a.m. alarm for the airport easier to handle.

They stood arm in arm on the banks of the Danube, their breaths visible in the crisp air. The river stretched before them, a ribbon of steel-grey water where chunks of ice danced across the surface, carried by the downstream current. Above them loomed the watchful gaze of the hilled fortress, its ancient stones a stark contrast to the city below, notably absent of modern skyscrapers.

The Irishwoman had made no mention of living together since their conversation went sour a month ago and Sophie was sure that she didn't remember even having it.

Hungary had not yet shed its winter chill, the air sharp enough to pinken their cheeks and noses. Seeking refuge from the cold, they ducked into a wine bar nestled down a cobblestone side street, its entrance marked only by a small, wrought-iron sign swinging gently in the breeze.

Inside, its red brick walls stretched towards a vaulted ceiling illuminated by the soft glow of candles poked into the necks of empty bottles. They perched on two stools, a small table between them, basking in the soft light and anonymity best found overseas.

"Tell me again, how did we end up here and not Venice?" Sarah asked, her eyes twinkling with amusement as she poured two glasses of deep red wine.

"Because you have an incredibly persuasive girlfriend who you love so dearly," Sophie said with a wink.

"That I do."

There was an anxiety that had grown over the months as the weight of her secret grew and her lies became more complex. But here, in this cosy nook of Budapest, with just the two of them, it seemed to vanish completely. There were no threats of eyes who might, on the off-chance, know somebody who knew somebody else. It was just her and Sophie, and that was all that mattered.

"Are you happy?" Sarah tilted her head to the side. "Honestly?"

"My answer doesn't change no matter how often you ask." Sophie gave her a toothy smile and took a sip of her drink while playfully watching her over the rim.

"I am too." Sarah reached over and took Sophie's hand, holding it tightly in her own. Their embrace lingered, fingers intertwined on the weathered wooden table.

It wouldn't have usually. Back home, there would be only brief grazes of their knees or fingers, a peck on the cheek unidentifiable as anything more to the average onlooker. No chance of it being misinterpreted, or indeed, interpreted correctly. It was their code, her code, showing affection only hidden from the outside world. But here, in this foreign city, Sarah allowed herself this moment.

How she wished that weekend would have lasted forever and to hold on to that feeling inside that felt like fireworks bursting. Any facade she kept had dropped. She had introduced Sophie openly as her partner, her girlfriend, to anybody she came into conversation with. As an Irishwoman, Sophie noticed, that seemed to happen a lot – her accent drew many strangers into conversation.

Three days they had spent dipping into hot sulphur baths and walking through winding streets packed with ornate and imposing buildings, their footsteps echoing on centuries-old cobblestones. Beautiful Gothic architecture surrounded them, spires and intricate stonework that would not have looked out of place in Florence or Paris.

The buzzing of Sarah's phone in her bag interrupted their moment outside Parliament earlier that afternoon, shattering the bubble of contentment they had built. She checked the screen, a picture of her mother's horrified face in front of a burnt turkey rousing a smile though she clicked 'answer' after spending all day declining. The real world, with all its complications and expectations, was intruding on their escape.

There was no obvious reason for it, but Sophie strongly suspected it was what Sarah didn't say that caused her to drop Sarah's hand and wander off alone.

"...no, no Mam, I'm just at a conference. Ah yes, I'm with Julia, we're just walking past Margaret Island now. It's that big bit in the middle of the river, and the bridge, you know? Ah no, never mind..."

Her words had been carried on the wind and irritatingly nipped at Sophie's ears. The truth was, Sophie knew Sarah's family was unaware of their relationship, but she hadn't considered the lies Sarah told in its place.

Sophie strolled along the river's edge, its surface reflecting the city's lights like shattered glass, the grand buildings lining the riverbank standing as silent witnesses to her inner turmoil. Each quiet denial of Sophie's existence in Sarah's life was a tiny dagger poking at her happiness, a signal that she was something easy to hide away. That she *should* be hidden away.

Another truth, which Sophie was becoming increasingly aware of, was a poisonous concoction of jealousy and doubt that had been slowly simmering inside of her. Almost an anger at living her life in suspension on the periphery of somebody else's.

Would Sarah ever admit to the people at the end of the phone who she was really sharing her life with? Or at what point would it all crumble beneath her feet? More than anything, Sophie despised her paralysis in taking control of the situation.

Sometimes in the moments of midnight wine-fuelled truths, Sarah would tell her, 'I will have got to sixty-five and not told a soul about us.' This trip to Budapest, with its thermal baths and Gothic spires, was partly Sophie's attempt to embed herself so deeply in Sarah's memory that she couldn't be denied, even if their relationship didn't last. It was selfish, almost childish, but never mentioned in the light of day when everything returned to 'normal'. Yet those words hung in the air like a rancid odour only Sophie could smell.

Then there were the Tinder notifications that Sophie pretended not to notice. Little red cancerous cells which latched onto Sophie and made her feel like a paranoid psychopath. They were there, on the right-hand side of the icon when Sarah flicked through her phone to show her something, and then the next time they were not. *Were they messages? Was she responding? Was she actively swiping?* She could not rid herself of these voices asking incessant questions and destabilising them both.

Sophie hadn't mentioned any of this to the girls; they were dubious enough about Sarah and she didn't need to add fuel to that particular fire. Their parroting opinions of 'you could do better', 'she's messing you around' and 'we don't like her – the sooner you see for yourself, the better' rang in her ears.

And so she found herself with nowhere to turn because nobody understood. They didn't see the way Sarah surprised her with tickets to the theatre and to dinner, with candlelit baths and home-cooked meals, the gentle caresses and warmth of her eyes, the sincerity of her actions which far outweighed the drunken doubts in the middle of the night that were words in the wind by morning.

"You've been quiet, my love. Are you tired?" Sarah returned to Sophie's side and pulled her out of her thoughts.

"Yeah, let's go," Sophie yawned.

Sarah found Sophie's hand and held it tight, as if fearing a strong wind might whisk her love away. They were a little drunk, but what a perfect night they'd had. Tomorrow, reality would set in again: a flight to London, Sophie's first week at work without Boozy Lauren to make it bearable.

Sophie nestled into the fresh white sheets of their bed which crinkled and rustled beneath her weight.

"Sophie, can I ask you something, seriously?" Sarah said, climbing into bed beside her.

"Mhmmm?" she responded lazily as dreams reached out to wind their arms around her waist. Sophie could feel her arms and legs sinking into the mattress as if they had already drifted off and were waiting for her head to follow.

"What are we going to do about us?" Sarah fiddled with the hem of the duvet.

"...I don't know, my love," came the response.

"But you know what I mean?"

"Mhmm, yes..." Sophie said, willing for the conversation to go away because she was scared at how it might finish.

"For God's sake, Sophie, just tell me what you're thinking!" Sarah demanded.

"I'm thinking that I want to go to fucking sleep," Sophie said, sitting bolt upright in bed and staring at Sarah, who looked back defiantly. "What do you want me to say that I haven't said a thousand times before?

No, I haven't entered this relationship completely blind. Yes, I know this is either going to go well or completely sodding pear-shaped. Do we really need to keep revisiting this discussion?"

The room seemed to close in around them and the Sandman had done a runner. All Sophie wanted was an uneventful night to end a pretty-perfect long weekend but there they were again; the clock was ticking towards midnight and Sarah's demons had come out to play.

Sarah's voice softened, tinged with a mixture of guilt and longing. "But it's not fair on you... when I dream about my future, it's not you. It's with people back home, and I think, 'Oh, that'd be nice...'"

Sophie sat motionless in the dark, her hand covering her mouth, staring at the lumps in the quilt where her knees had tensed into cotton pyramids. The beautiful city of Budapest, with its thermal baths and Gothic spires, suddenly felt a million miles away. Whatever glimmer of possibility she had harboured over the past eight months was extinguished, like the lights of the city outside their window being snuffed out one by one.

"Look, I know that's what you've always had in your head," Sophie said softly, thankful that the darkness hid the salty tears she could feel running down her cheeks, "and I know you beat yourself up about falling in love with a woman. But please, let's have this conversation another time."

"How do you know I do?" asked Sarah.

"Because this isn't the first time we've had this discussion, or even the second." Sophie willed herself not to sniff; it would only cause Sarah to turn on the light and see she was crying.

They were overdue a discussion propelled by Sarah's doubts; she just wished it hadn't happened there. Each time her doubts reared their ugly heads and fuelled such a conversation, Sophie held out hope that Sarah would at least remember it the next day. It felt grossly unfair that only she would carry the weight of the words that sporadically stained their relationship.

Those words tormented her at each opportunity. When she was alone at night, or when Tinder popped up, or when Aoife and Morag rang Sarah because she knew everything about them but they didn't even know who or what she was.

"Maybe, you know," Sarah said, "in two or three years, we could be friends... I don't want to lose you from my life."

Sophie paused.

"There will be no friendship after this ends, Sarah," she said, surprised by the hollowness in her voice as if she'd had to prise the words from her mouth, but Sarah had already fallen asleep.

Her soft snoring soon filled the room, oblivious to the audible breaking of Sophie's heart. The moonlight, once romantic, now felt harsh and exposing as it illuminated Sarah's honey-coloured curls fanned out on the white pillow.

Stupid, stupid, stupid girl, what have you done? The tears would not stop now and a herd of elephants would not wake Sarah.

Sophie blindly groped in the night for her book and retreated to the armchair under the window. The room was cold now, but she preferred the goosebumps to prickle her skin and set her hairs on end than to be in bed with Sarah. Tears fell rapidly on the pages before her body gave way to shock and convulsed in silent sobs.

Half of her wanted – no, *willed* – Sarah to wake up and see the damage she had done, to take some responsibility. She stared into the abyss, wishing she had fallen asleep long before this discussion began. It was a hard admonition that her dreams of them were just that; dreams.

A seismic shift had taken place and the first brick from the bridge had fallen into the valley below. She had hope for them, a tiny and powerful flicker that had carried her through the darkest of nights, but now that light was gone.

Chapter Twenty-One

"You cannot project-manage your break-up," said Lauren in a voice tinged with exasperation.

They were nestled in the Blues Kitchen off Kingsland Road, Lauren's new local haunt. They started the evening with the determination to be sensible and have only a glass of wine apiece; until Sophie finished recounting her trip, at which point Lauren saw fit to order a bottle for 'medicinal reasons.'

The taxi ride to the airport the day they left Budapest was a study in forced normality. Sophie was notably distant and spent most of the ride staring out of the rain-flecked windows at the blue-grey blur of the city flying past them.

Sarah didn't seem to remember anything of the night after they got back to their hotel room, and thought she would give Sophie space with her thoughts and dive into her inbox. She was now working abroad for two weeks, and though they spoke daily, Sophie couldn't help but let the distance between them grow.

Little did she know that Sarah was itching to come to London, and home to Sophie.

"Watch me," Sophie responded and topped up their glasses. Their time was up, she had decided. While she had been happy to go with the flow and let Sarah call the shots, she never wanted to feel so humiliated again. Their break-up would now be on her terms.

She spoke with Gennaro that week. As far as he was concerned, there was a family situation keeping her in the UK which wasn't a complete untruth, but that situation was almost resolved and she would be free to move, though not right away.

She had it all planned.

It would be a Friday night. Not midweek – she needed her sleep – and not a Saturday either because she'd need more than a Sunday to wallow before going back to work. No, a Friday night would allow her the weekend.

She'd go to Sarah's and pop her jacket on the back of the sofa near the door – close enough to grab it and go, but not so unusual that Sarah would immediately notice something was wrong.

Sarah would bring two glasses of wine over to the sofa which Sophie wouldn't drink, because she'd need to keep a clear head if she was to stick to her resolve. At which point Sarah would notice there was something Sophie needed to say and then they'd have 'the talk'.

The thought of Sarah crying was a heartbreak in itself but deep down, they both knew it was for the best.

Except Sarah returned to London earlier than planned.

Her last meeting of the week had been unexpectedly cancelled. It was supposed to be an all-day affair of schmoozing with contractors and in-tense discussions about the price of scaffolding, which she was thankful to have avoided.

As she settled into her seat on the plane, a mixture of relief, antici-pation, and gnawing guilt churned in her stomach. The past two weeks had been a whirlwind of meetings punctuated by increasingly persistent phone calls from her mother, and she wanted nothing more than to be at home with Sophie.

"But Sarah, darling," her mother had said just that morning, "you're not getting any younger. What about that nice Murphy boy? He's a doctor now, you know."

Sarah had sighed, her patience wearing thin. "Mam, I'm seeing someone."

"Oh?" Her mother's interest was piqued immediately. "Who is he? What does he do?"

In a moment of panic, Sarah had blurted out, "His name is Sam. He's... he's in finance." The lie had tasted bitter on her tongue, but it had the desired effect of momentarily silencing her mother's matchmaking efforts.

Now, as the plane descended into London, Sarah felt awful about the fabrication. She hadn't meant to invent a male alter ego for Sophie, but the pressure of her mother's expectations and her own unresolved feelings had pushed her into a corner. The lies were piling up, and Sarah felt an urgent need to ease her conscience by creating a more comprehensive 'cover' for her secret relationship.

Then again, she reasoned, it might be a beneficial lie. Not only would it discourage Finnoula's haphazard matchmaking efforts – proffering her daughter to any eligible man she came across, either directly or indirectly – but later down the line she could turn Sam into Sophie.

Maybe after some years of Sophie being 'Sam', and her family seeing how happy she was with him, would they be more accepting of 'him' actually being a 'her'.

It still made her nervous to think of her Mum making a spontaneous trip to London and demanding to meet this mysterious man of whom

Sarah spoke so highly. She'd have to come up with a plan, and fast, to manage these potential situations without hurting Sophie.

Sarah's thoughts drifted to their recent weekend in Budapest, a bittersweet memory now tainted by her growing web of deception. The memory of Sophie's smile as they walked along the Danube, the warmth of her hand as they explored the city's winding streets, the soft sound of her breathing as they fell asleep in their hotel room – all of it filled Sarah with a longing that was now mixed with apprehension.

Sophie had been withdrawn in the car to the airport and for their journey home. Sarah supposed she wasn't alone in the apprehension about the lies that engulfed them and their imminent return to reality. Conversations with her girlfriend over the past two weeks had been frequent yet brief, extending no further than pleasantries and a quick debrief before they were interrupted by either a call from her mother or from work, which didn't help the distance she felt between them.

Though it was always a comfort to hear Sophie's voice. Even more so to see her face and feel the warmth of her skin.

The sky over London had opened up, unleashing a torrential downpour. As the taxi pulled up to her building, she could barely make out the familiar facade through the sheets of rain cascading down the windows.

"Bloody hell," Sarah muttered, fumbling in her bag for an umbrella she knew wasn't there. With a resigned sigh, she paid the driver and braced herself for the inevitable soaking.

Cold droplets pelted her face and neck, quickly seeping through her light jacket. Her carefully styled hair, which had survived the flight intact, now plastered itself to her forehead and cheeks in dark, sodden strands.

Her keys slipped from her wet fingers twice before she managed to unlock the front door. Her suitcase bumped and scraped against each step, the noise echoing in the empty stairwell. Finally reaching her flat, Sarah fumbled with her keys again, leaving wet smears on the door as she struggled to find the right one. As she pushed the door open, she was met with darkness and silence.

All she wanted now was to have a hot shower, fresh clothes and for Sophie to come over. Maybe they'd open a bottle of wine, order in from that Thai place Sophie loved...

When Sophie arrived, their greeting was brief and tense. They kissed quickly, and Sophie's coat was draped over the sofa – a detail that would later feel significant. Sarah handed Sophie a glass of wine, which barely touched her lips before being set down on the table.

As they sat down, Sarah sensed something was amiss. Sophie's body language was closed off, her eyes avoiding direct contact. Sarah's heart rate quickened as she realised this wasn't going to be the cosy evening she had envisioned.

"I sense we need to talk about something," Sarah said, her voice quiet but steady.

Sophie nodded, finally meeting Sarah's gaze. "Yes."

Sarah twirled the stem of her wine glass between her fingers and pulled her lips into a grimace before looking at Sophie with glassy red eyes. Sophie felt sick with nerves.

"I don't want this to be a secret, but I can't, I just can't..." Sarah's voice faltered, unexpectedly taking the lead in the conversation.

Sophie, though she had initiated this discussion, found herself caught off guard by Sarah's response. She challenged, "Tell me – why can't you?"

"I can't," Sarah said, offering no further explanation.

"That's not an answer," Sophie pressed. She could see the internal struggle in Sarah's eyes – the desire to be happy and loved warring with the fear of what that love might cost her.

A heavy silence fell between them, both of them too stubborn to break it.

Finally, Sophie continued, her voice gaining strength as she spoke. "I'll tell you why you think you can't. You're worried what people are going to think of you because they've known you to be with men all your life, and now, out of the blue, you fall in love with a woman. You're worried how people will speak about you.

But here's what I've learnt through coming out," she continued, undeterred, "if they're as good friends as you count them to be, and if they loved you like they say, if they had any modicum of respect for you at all, they wouldn't care. And if they do, then they aren't your friends.

Sarah McCarthy, you are nearly forty years old and you have to stop living your life to make other people happy because I can tell you now, they do not do that for you. They do not stop living their lives wondering whether you'll approve of what makes them happy, so why do you?"

The words kept coming, spilling from her lips like semantic diarrhoea, and none of it was in the script. Even Craig knew the script. He could stand and recite it while cleaning his teeth.

"You lay next to me in bed and you cup my face... my face with your hand and you tell me that you're the happiest you've ever been, so why do you want to give that up for people who don't matter? You cannot play the martyr forever."

"You're right," Sarah said simply. "Then why are you still here?"

"Because, firstly, I love you. And secondly because I know that neither of this ever expected this, us, to happen. And I understand that, I understand your fear because you've never been in this situation and to be honest, neither have I. But I know that I don't want to leave you, even though I think I need to."

"Tell me, are you hurting?"

"Yes." Sophie could feel the lump in her throat.

"You're going to cry."

"I know, this is precisely why I've avoided this conversation in the past, because it's usually always happened when we've had a drink."

"Are you hurting badly?"

"Yes," Sophie whispered.

"I'm sorry. I'm so sorry."

"Please stop saying that word, because when you say it nothing changes and I believe it less the next time around."

A cold cloud rose and manifested between the two, an atmosphere sliced by Sarah's hands reaching out for Sophie's face and pulling it forward until it was three inches from her own. Soul-searching eyes bore deep.

"I feel like..." Sophie took a deep breath to steady her thundering heart and quaking voice. "That I'm only here until you meet somebody else – a man – who you can take home... to your parents. And I am... sick... of feeling like... I am not good enough for you."

"Do you want me to be taking you home to Ireland, is that it?" Sarah asked with her eyebrows pushed together.

"It's not going to happen, is it?"

Sarah paused, her eyes cast downward as she pulled away and placed her hands deliberately on her lap. "No. I'm sorry, but I can never, ever tell anybody."

Sophie's feet stirred, as if they had heard their cue and now knew it was time to be moving. A surge of emotion welled up inside her as she sat upright, wiping the tears from her face with trembling fingers. "Then I need to leave," she said, her voice barely above a whisper.

"No!" Sarah shouted, bewildered. "Is that what you want?"

Sophie felt a surge of frustration rising within her. "Wait, you don't want me to go, but you don't want me to be more than I am? So tell me, what on earth do you want me to sit here and say?"

The rage was coming now, a stark contrast to the slow, puny tears that had fallen before. The anger began to bubble up, and the pent-up frustration arrived like a pan of overboiling starchy water. God, it felt glorious to finally let it out.

"No. You are not walking out of that door. I won't allow it." Sarah leapt to her feet, grasping Sophie's wrist with desperate intensity. She opened her mouth to speak, but her voice faltered, cracking with emotion. "I'm just struggling... I can't, I can't accept myself... I need time. Please, I need more time. I love you. I love you so much. I just need... time. But please, please my love, don't go."

In her two weeks of meticulous planning and mental dress rehearsals, this was not an outcome Sophie had prepared for. Not once had she entertained the possibility that Sarah would beg her to reconsider. She stopped in her tracks, frozen by the sight of Sarah's knees giving way as her entire body melted onto the sofa in shuddering sobs.

Her anger swept away by shock, Sophie wanted nothing more than to wrap her arms around the delicate body curled in her shame and to tell her everything would be all right, she would be fine. And that's exactly what she did, because in spite of the unfairness of the situation, that woman meant more to Sophie than anything she had ever known. She loved her with everything she had, and she needed her to believe in them.

That night, two lovers lay in a tangle of limbs, their bodies intertwined despite the sweaty humidity growing under the duvet. They remained bound by their stubborn refusal to leave the safe sanctuary they had created in each other's arms.

Chapter Twenty-Two

Neatly manicured nails raked through honey-coloured curls before coming to rest on the crown of her head. The streetlamps lining the Gran Vía glowed in the blackened sky, their light transforming into streaks and smears. Rain hammered against the glass, splintering the street into dots of red, white, and orange that bled together and trickled down towards the pavement below.

She was dizzy. She closed her eyes but that made it worse. The voices of drunk ghosts rushed past her ears in excitable chatter like the rush of a violent wind carrying waves of laughter and Irish voices through the bar. Her phone said it was eleven p.m. but it felt much later.

"It's your round, Sarah." Aoife's hand landed heavily on her back. "C'mon, I'll help you carry them."

The bar was dark and dimly lit. It was a local favourite that Morag had ferreted out after spending an ungodly number of hours planning the perfect hen party, much as she'd done for Sarah in the past. A stab of shame struck her as she thought of how those efforts had gone to waste. Yet, what a weekend they'd had – two exhilarating days whizzing around Lisbon, drinking enough Vinho Verde to sink a merchant ship.

A group of men stood beside the bar, the only other people in there. They were slightly younger than her; Sarah placed them in their mid-thirties and the shortest was just under six foot tall. In a rugged way they were quite charming and by the sound of it, they were Irish too.

From the toilets emerged a blond man and the group of a dozen men fell about in fits of laughter. He wore a bridal veil over his face and had lipstick smudged about his mouth.

"I'd make a crap woman," she heard him say on returning.

"Listen, Michael," said the tallest of the men, his hair swept back into a quiff, leaning on the shoulder of the man in the veil. "I've just farted and I'm going to need you to take the blame or those lovely ladies at the bar here are going to think it was me."

"You're a dirty bastard, John, of course I'm not." He laughed and looked over before staggering a few steps backwards.

"Steady there now, or you'll end up in a ditch and the last time you did that, you got the news you were going to be a father four weeks later." The group roared with laughter.

The black-haired one, Carl, piped up. "Hey, if his missus hears you've slandered her good name then we're all in for a beating."

"Ah, I'm only joking, Colleen knows I adore the bones of her." John picked up his pint from the bar and winked at Aoife, who had turned her back to Sarah to face them.

"Careful now, not as much as I do." Michael straightened himself and took a swig from his empty pint glass before realising there was no beer left.

"Do I detect Dublin accents?" Aoife asked.

"Wahey, they're Irish!" Carl cheered and pulled out his wallet. "Here girls, get yerselves a drink there, on me."

"Hold on now, unless you want to buy a drink for those fourteen other lovely ladies over there I'd suggest you put that away now or you'll be out of pocket." Sarah chuckled. "But thank you anyway."

"Well, can I at least ask your names?"

"I'm Aoife, she's Sarah and we're both single."

"Jesus Chris, Aoife, do you want to go telling them our addresses while you're at it?" Sarah said, growing red.

Laughter from the other side of the bar bounced off the whitewashed walls and terracotta floor. The hens hadn't noticed two of their flock had caught the attention of the cocks at the bar.

"So, ladies, if you don't have boyfriends," Michael began, setting down his still-empty glass and putting his arms around Paul and John, "I have two fine fellas in mind if you're interested."

"Ah, get lost with you." Sarah said, jovially batting the offer to one side. "I've got drinks to order still. We'll have a very thirsty bridal party on our hands if I don't."

"Now, Sarah, let us not dismiss these nice lads so quickly," Aoife playfully chided as she gave their muscular frames a once-over.

"Excuse me, can we have two bottles of cava, and ten gin and tonics please?" Sarah turned to the bartender and busied herself sorting through her purse. They were attractive, Aoife had a point; they would usually be her type. She could hear Aoife wheedling their life stories from them. Worked in finance, own flats, Carl actually lived in London – 'feasible for Sarah', she could hear her say. *No, no, not feasible for Sarah*, she thought but she couldn't say.

Sarah turned with the first tray of drinks and headed back to her own party.

"Miss McCarthy, you come here now." Sarah heard Aoife clatter after her.

"What's got her back up?" Morag asked, unloading the first half-dozen gins and handing them around the group.

"What are you playing at, woman?" Aoife demanded, her voice a mixture of exasperation and concern. "You've just had two gorgeous men offered to you on a plate and you do a runner. And I'd have even let you choose first and taken whoever was left over."

"How charitable of you," Morag said drily, her sarcasm a familiar comfort to Sarah.

"I just – I wasn't in the mood," Sarah said.

"Well, the only way you'll carry on riding is if you get back on the horse. You probably need a good riding." Aoife pulled a packet of salty crisps from her clutch bag, her eyes glinting with mischief.

"Aoife, please, we're in public. A lot of people understand what you're saying," Morag rebuked, her gaze darting nervously to an older couple who had just entered the bar. They had clearly overheard the comment, their eyes widening in shock.

"Now I spy a group of men in here well up for a laugh. You'd better up your game, McCarthy, or we'll be having more words. C'mon, let's have a laugh with these eejits dressed like the fuckin' Spice Girls."

Despite the impressive amount she'd spent on gin and wine, sleep still evaded Sarah. She lay alone in the dark, dreams of Sophie invading her consciousness in broken bursts of restless slumber.

In her dreams, she found herself at home on a hill, the rolling green fields beneath her feet stretching out to meet an expansive blue noth-ingness in the distance. Warm hands wrapped around her waist, fingers threading together over a swollen stomach. Soft lips whispered fleeting kisses down her neck.

Hand in hand, they walked barefoot into the house of her parents. But the moment of bliss was shattered as her parents cast one look at them and turned them away. The room began to spin, the house disap-peared and suddenly they were back on the hill. Heavy rain came down like arrows of judgement, their clothes clinging desperately to cold skin whipped by the bitter winds of the harsh sea.

'You are no daughter of mine.'

'How could you do this to our family?'

'Do you hear what people are saying about you?'

'How can you walk down the street?'

'The shame of it, can you believe?'

When she woke, her sheets were sodden with sweat, the room bathed in a harsh light with only tulle drapes to block its crude intrusion. Sarah heaved a heavy sigh, summoned from the tips of her toes, and flopped backwards onto the bed. She wanted to go home.

Chapter Twenty-Three

Craig raised his glass and drained the dregs. Reaching for the bottle in the middle of the table only to find it empty, he exhaled loudly, a sound of genuine loss and woe.

"I'll take the hint that it's my round," Sophie said sarcastically and got up to occupy the empty spot at the bar.

The L-shaped room had its original corner bar, tall and polished with brass accoutrements. A faded carpet, once red, brown and beige, had worn with age to a multicoloured mass of brown tones. Wingback leather armchairs cracked with the decades nestled among dark wood chairs with spindle backs and red velvet seat cushions tied to their bases.

On this last weekend before payday, as the population of the city confined themselves to their flats or scrounged for coppers to buy their drinks, the pub was quiet. The gentle ambience was soon shattered as Boozy Lauren made an entrance, crashing through the door with her arms aloft, cheering herself.

"Sophie!" she almost shouted and threw her arms around her neck.

"Have you been drinking already?" Craig asked, tearing his eyes from the dark-haired man with the Mediterranean tan and tight jeans leaning against the bar to turn and eye Lauren suspiciously.

"No!" Lauren laughed, her eyes sparkling with mirth. "Sorry I'm late though, I missed my train because I was watching these two women at

Euston trying to lift a life-sized papier-mâché sarcophagus onto the train to Hemel Hempstead."

Sophie laughed.

"So, Lauren," Craig shamelessly steered the conversation towards his own interests, lest it travel further down the route of DIY death rituals, "the man at the bar with the tan and tight arse, is he on your team or mine?"

"Mine. Definitely. Without a shadow of a doubt," she said, running her eyes up and down the man's body appreciatively. "I think I'll go for a drink and find out. You're drinking wine, yeah?"

"See, why didn't you do that instead of hungrily ogle him from afar?" Sophie nudged Craig as he stared aghast as Lauren sidled up beside his fantasy boyfriend. In his head, he'd already planned their wedding, decided what house they'd buy, and chosen their children's names. "This is why my dad calls her a sexual predator. She didn't even sit down first."

"But Sophie, staring hungrily over the bar is gay flirting. Watch each other, pretend you're not, hope that they're more confident than you are and go home and cry into your pillow when neither of you speak," Craig protested, turning his attention back to his empty glass. "I like to think of my dating history as a little more sophisticated than dragging drunk men from the streets."

Yet that is exactly where that particular Friday evening took him. Despite Lauren's best efforts, Andreas the Greek, as they had named him, interrupted their conversation to ask her more about the 'colourful man with glasses and beard', and so she returned to the table and sent Craig up in her place.

"Do you remember when you dated somebody Greek?" Lauren said, sitting down in Craig's warm chair and plonking another bottle of wine in the ice bucket.

"Yes... and it turned out she spent the entire relationship hooked on ketamine," Sophie said drily, cracking the screw cap open.

"I can't believe you didn't realise that was the reason she kept falling asleep in her dinner." Lauren laughed and slapped the table.

"Well, it's hardly the first thing that comes to mind, you know." Sophie chuckled. "I just couldn't believe it when she said, 'I feel like that's the reason you dumped me. You know, because of the gear.' Erm, no shit, Sherlock!"

"Speaking of dumping..." Lauren said. "How long do you think it's going to be before you want to end it with Sarah again?"

Sophie paused. The truth was, while she believed in Sarah's desire to make their relationship work, a nagging doubt lingered in the recesses of her mind. She wasn't wholly convinced that Sarah would see it through.

But then, a more pressing question arose: how long should one give a situation like this? Sophie knew she couldn't – wouldn't – force Sarah to come out. That was a deeply personal journey, one that Sarah needed to take in her own time, when she felt good and ready.

Gennaro was in Florence poised to welcome her into his team. He was only waiting on an email to tell him when she had her flights booked. She wished she'd planned for Sarah to fight for their relationship because now she wasn't sure what to do.

As the days turned into weeks, and weeks into months, Sophie found herself grappling with a difficult reality. How long could she really stay in the shadows and be happy about it? Or perhaps more accurately, how long could she remain accepting of this half-life, this love that had to remain hidden?

"Oh, Sophie, I'm having such a great time!" Sarah sang down the phone.

Sophie couldn't help but think that Sarah sounded better than she felt. It was the day before the Directors' meeting where they would walk around the new site with the developers, approve the menu, and review the figures for their existing four restaurants. And just now, her computer had crashed with everything on it. Did she save it? It was auto-saving, surely, that was the point of the cloud. But does that work when the blue screen of death arrives without warning? These thoughts raced through Sophie's mind as she tried to maintain her composure.

"I'm glad you did." Sophie responded in a manner calmer than she felt. "Your friends sound mental though, I'd have died and somebody would have ended up calling my mam."

Sarah's laughter crackled through the phone. "I tell you what, we met the biggest group of bollocks on Saturday night. They were there on a lads' holiday and dressed up like the Spice Girls. Anyway, this one silly bollocks had a bit of cocaine on him so asked if I wanted a little bit too. Well, everybody else was on it, so I thought what's the harm? So we just went into a cubicle and then he tried to kiss me! I said 'Oh no, no thanks. I'm only here for the cocaine, you see.' Then I had a line and ran off."

Sophie paused for a second, thankful that Sarah was not there in person to witness her half-smile and furrowed brow. Or to question what was wrong because she wasn't entirely sure herself. There was something in that sentence that made her breath catch in her throat.

It's not like she did anything, Sophie, she ran off. Then again, surely his intention was pretty clear when he invited her into a cubicle...

You should trust her, she thought, half-fearing that all it would take to end them would be one lapse in judgement or misunderstanding and it would be game over.

"Anyway, I've got to go now. I can hear Aoife banging on the door and she's wanting to say hello to my Mam who she thinks I'm on the phone to. Love you," She whispered hurriedly and ended the call.

Inhale. I am a calm and tranquil person. Exhale. I am Zen, I am whole. Inhale. I do not need to be angry. Exhale. I am beyond anger. Inhale. I am an ethereal being with no violent thoughts towards this laptop.

Exhale.

Longer.

Longer.

Keep exhaling.

I am a calm and tranquil person with no angry thoughts, she repeated.

She peeled one eye open, pupils pierced by the harsh cobalt light of her screen which affirmed that her work was, indeed, gone, and she would be up all night trying to either fix it or rewrite everything. She cried out in frustration, inclined to put her fist right through the fucking—

Sophie, breathe, you lunatic! Inhale. Exhale. Inhale. Exhale.

She kicked herself across the metal floor, the wheels of her chair noisily clunking over the cracks and reverberating around the empty office. "Please, please, please." She put her head in her hands because the alternative was doing something regrettable to company property and she certainly did not want to give Hector a reason to lose his temper, again. Only earlier that day had he taken his shoe off and launched it over their new restaurant, taking out two glass deer. A temper tantrum that cost five thousand pounds they didn't have, a headache and a sous chef in tears.

"Sophie, what—" Ana, Hector's assistant, appeared at the main door. "Are you OK?"

"Oh, sorry, I didn't realise anybody else was here," Sophie said apologetically, suddenly aware of her outburst.

"Yes, I gathered." She smiled. "You were saying 'fuck' rather a lot."

"I've just lost the budget sheets and Directors' presentations for to-morrow morning, so... I've been better." Sophie peeked through her fingers at the woman smiling understandingly back at her.

And my girlfriend just happened to spend time with a random man in a toilet cubicle over the weekend and I'm not sure whether there's more to it or not, she thought about saying but wouldn't dream of it.

"I'm actually here to find out what your diary is like next Friday?" Ana said with a subtle Latin American accent, her tongue rolling around her Rs. Even Lauren had fancied Ana when she joined a couple of years ago; she had the sun-kissed glow of a woman who grew up with the sun as a consistent being rather than it being a special event that came between weeks of rain and cloud.

"Before I answer that, will there be food?" Sophie half-pleaded.

"The best I can do is buy you a packet of crisps from the vending machine, then lock you in the room with Hector?" Ana offered and shrugged.

"Fine, book it in." She sighed. Between her computer crisis, Sarah's revelations, and the prospect of being locked in a room with Hector, she wondered if the universe was testing her patience.

"Oh, and by the way," Ana poked her head back around, "did you know that your jumper is see-through?"

Chapter Twenty-Four

A soft finger crept down the inside of Sophie's forearm, swirling and caressing her wrist before dancing around the palm of her hand and being playfully snatched away. The owner of those soft hands grinned at her from the other side of the gravel path to which she had retreated.

Leaves bleached white with hot sun danced in the faint breeze that skimmed the ripples of the river before whistling up the trunks of cedar trees which towered overhead and rustled in satisfaction. Sophie took shelter in the long shadows they cast along the limestone path they lined. Any day that saw the slightest hint of sunlight meant that she would be dousing herself with aftersun and retreating to bed that evening a not-so-delightful shade of lobster, then spending the following days hoping it might turn into some semblance of a tan.

"We probably should stay at yours for the next few days, if that's all right?" Sarah asked. "Helen needs a bit of space from us."

"That's fair, I'd like to cook in my own kitchen for a couple of nights anyway. What should I make for us?" Sophie hummed contentedly.

"How do you turn the subject of any conversation back to food?" Sarah laughed.

"It's a talent of mine." Sophie smiled in return, a gaze Sarah held with a broad grin that reached her eyes so they sparkled in the light.

On warm mid-spring days, where the mercury rose high enough to pique London's excitement with the promise of summer. Shorts and sandals were dug from the bottoms of wardrobes, sunglasses pulled from dressing tables and sun-hats, none of which had seen the light of day since early September, fished from the top shelf and promptly carted down to the closest park or pub.

A ringing in the far distance grew steadily louder. Following it was the laughter of small voices and tyres crunching on stone as two blonde-haired children on pink and purple bikes rocketed past with an apologetic parent in tow.

That's going to be me one day, apologising to pedestrians my kids have terrorised, Sophie thought.

"I'm still struggling, you know," Sarah said as if she had read her mind and sensed Sophie was getting ahead of herself.

"I know, my love, it's not easy. Is it?" Sophie gave her arm a subtle squeeze.

"The way I see this, is… is that I'm the most horrible person and I make you feel like utter shit," Sarah said.

She meant it too. How could anybody in their right mind want to be with somebody on the cusp of forty and be kept in the shadows like a terrible secret? She didn't understand it. If she were in that situation, she'd tell whoever was doing it to go to hell and leave without a care. But Sophie never did. Sophie didn't raise her voice, she didn't shout, she didn't scream, she just sat there. It wasn't fair for her to be doing what she was to somebody like that.

"No, you don't," Sophie replied almost breathlessly, as if she was trying to beg for the conversation to come to a close before it really ever begun. As if she pleaded enough in her intonation that Sarah would get the hint and not darken the memory of their Saturday morning walk with a serious conversation where one did not belong.

"Then tell me." Sarah took up the challenge. "Tell me how I make you feel. I've not met your friends, or your parents either and it's been nine months, surely they have expectations – and you too – but I don't know if I can meet them. I'm scared that I can't."

"All my parents care about is whether I'm happy or not. And I am, that's all that matters. They don't have any expectations." Sophie said. "I don't either. It's best not to have any or..."

"Sure you do," Sarah pushed.

"No..." Sophie paused, wondering how it was most diplomatic to say 'I want a life with you but I don't expect it to happen or I'll be horribly disappointed if, or when, this comes to an end and I don't want to be left a fool for hoping for something that could never happen.' "I don't expect anything, because when we started we agreed to see how things went between us..."

Why was she avoiding the question? Sarah wondered.

"But you aren't telling me how you feel." Sarah pressed. "I genuinely don't think I can tell anybody. I've tried telling my best friends but the words... the words just... they get caught up and won't come out."

"I see..." Sophie replied, her voice carefully neutral.

"I know I'm hurting you by saying this, but I wish you'd just tell me that."

They walked in silence a while as Sophie gathered her thoughts, listening to the gentle padding of runners' feet passing by. Small stones ground together and crackled with each step on the walk from Putney to Battersea. Bushes stirred with the promise of life within. The crowd in Fulham stadium released a collective roar of joy which could be heard for a mile around.

"All right then, 'expectation' isn't the word," Sarah continued. "What is 'enough'? Is 'enough' continuing for another six months, six years?"

Sophie let the question hang in the air for a moment or two. More children rocketed past, followed by a running group led by dogs on leads. Dalmatians and labradors, blonde, brown and black, padded past with the smaller dogs in their wake.

"I think... there are two types of enough," Sophie began, her voice careful and measured. "The first is that we come to a mutual decision to end our relationship because it will never be more than what it is now. The second type of 'enough' is that we actually see a future for this, for us, and we fight for it. But to come to the decision of which route we take, you need to ask yourself whether you are prepared to tell people about me, not now, but in the future because I cannot exist like this forever."

"A future? What does that consist of – six years? Ten years?" Sarah scrutinised Sophie's face, her eyes narrowing slightly.

Don't say it, Sophie. Don't say it, the voice in her head pleaded.

"A forever kind of future," she said softly, ignoring the internal warning.

Sarah was looking at her; Sophie could feel her brown eyes boring into the side of her head, but she had her own eyes fixed to the yellow sandstone path and refused to meet them.

"What do you mean by that, though?" Sarah pressed, her voice a mixture of curiosity and apprehension.

"What do you think I mean by that?" Sophie snapped, her composure slipping. "A life, a future, marriage, children, all those things you want too."

It was the heat of the moment, a quick snap response she had promised to keep to herself and really wished she had. She wanted the ground to open up and swallow her whole rather than stand beside Sarah as she picked holes in her stupidity.

A soft 'oh' escaped Sarah's lips. She was dumbfounded. Sophie began to panic. *Shit, bastard, bollocks.* She shouldn't have said it, she should not have delivered it that way either. She might as well have screamed, 'I want to fucking marry you,' in front of the children's playground in Battersea.

"You know," Sophie continued quietly after conceding that if she was in for a penny, she may as well be in for a pound, "I never wanted children until I started to think about it a month or two ago. I never understood it when people used to tell me that if you find a person you love enough, then the idea arrives, and it sticks…"

Sophie pressed on, her words tumbling out now that the floodgates had opened. "And I remember the moment when I realised that I'd be a great parent. It felt like everything clicked. You were asleep, and my thoughts ran away with me and I thought what an amazing mother you'll be one day. You're so kind, and generous and gentle, and I always wanted to be with somebody who had those qualities, but fierce and independent too.

And I told myself it was dangerous, thinking this way would only get me into trouble but I don't think I'd have dared if I didn't believe that you loved me in that way too. But the thing is, I don't expect this to happen. I never have. I hope, I still hope, and I can't give up until there's no hope left."

Sarah said nothing. *Oh, you've really screwed it now, Soph.* But she'd said her piece; if this was the time where they had to draw a line in the sand and walk away, she was ready. There was no way she could look back and wish she had done more, had said more, and then perhaps things would have worked out differently.

"Look, Sarah," Sophie rubbed her face with her hands. The longer the silence persevered, the more she worried. "I'm sorry. It was too much. I shouldn't have said anything."

"How many children do you want?" Sarah asked simply, her voice surprisingly calm.

"Two, I think. I liked growing up with a brother."

"Me too." Sarah closed her eyes briefly and exhaled through her lips. She did that often, especially when she was concentrating, or trying to calm herself down. "Where would we live?"

"Not in London. Somewhere else."

"Home?"

"Yours or mine?"

"Either, I'm not bothered."

Sarah reached over the gap between them as they walked side by side but worlds apart until then, when she took her girlfriend's hand and weaved her fingers through Sophie's. The wind picked up and carried the hems of their skirts. It raced down the path picking up debris in its course, twisting and turning through long grass and overgrown weeds that spilled out through steel railings of abandoned warehouses and onto the towpath.

"I'd like that," the Irishwoman smiled. To Sophie, loving her was simple, yet devilishly complex because she did not think she deserved to be loved. So they decided to walk on the tightrope between dreams and reality, still wondering whether they'd make it to the other side; but decidedly, and most importantly, they did it together.

Chapter Twenty-Five

The smell of warm woodchip rose into the air, evoking fond memories of adventure playgrounds, water fountains and jelly sandals. It was an unseasonably warm early autumn day, and London had decided to make the most of a very brief second summer. Silky plumes of smoke billowed into the air from back-garden fire pits across Kensal Rise, creating a soft haze frolicking children squealing in unadulterated delight. It was undoubtedly an unexpected yet momentous occasion, after many months of failed negotiation, that two significant parties in Sophie's life would meet for the first time.

She had reassured Sarah with certainty that everything would be fine, and that Maria and Lauren specifically would play nicely. But it was a certainty that not even Sophie was certain about. By the nature of being Spanish, Maria had been aggrieved and insulted by Sarah's unwillingness to meet her.

'If we are important to you, meeting us should be important to her,' she had said. Often, actually. Lauren was a little more laid-back but no more likely to give Sarah an easy time. Nevertheless, Sophie sent a silent prayer to a deity of uncertain character, nature and existence, and hoped for the best.

It was every man, woman and child for themselves in the supermarket aisles, where every inhabitant within a two-mile radius of Ladbroke Grove fearlessly battled for the last of the barbecue supplies. Toddlers were tethered to wheels to make them easier to manoeuvre through the throngs of flip-flop-wearing, midriff-exposing, mildly pink people, pushing and shoving out of the way.

Sarah was convinced that the key to a good first impression lay within a bowl of potato salad large enough for an infant to bathe in. A dish she was so intent on preparing that she did not notice Craig striding into the kitchen, a feast for the eyes in an outfit that made him look like the love child of Ronald McDonald and Barney the Dinosaur.

"Do you like?" He held his palms aloft and twirled into the kitchen, a kaleidoscopic vision of pineapple print, pink and yellow. His beard had been trimmed to within an inch of its life and his brown curly hair had been cut and styled for the first time in months.

"Those jeans are so tight I can tell you've been circumcised," Sophie said, turning her attention back to the tomatoes.

"I figured since my life is so boring then my clothes needn't be."

"And because you always dressed so demurely before?" Sarah smiled innocently.

A thundering at the door ripped through the flat. Boozy Lauren could be the only cause of such a noise.

"I'll get that," Sophie said before slipping past the Banana-Coloured Wonder and scampering down the hallway.

"Sophie!" Lauren bellowed as if she were stood at the bottom of the path rather than right in front of her, and threw her arms around Sophie's neck in an unusual display of affection. Maria and Kirsten followed, carrying loud orange bags that clinked as they walked.

Lauren was the first of the trio to make a beeline for the kitchen, giving Craig only a cursory hello, much to his chagrin.

"Jesus, Sophie. How much food do you have in here?" said Kirsten, staring at the worktops covered in cucumbers, tomatoes and piles of burgers, sausages, marinating chicken and pork chops.

"You've got enough food to feet the Latvian army, mate," Lauren said, throwing her coat onto the sofa and introducing herself to Sarah. "And what the fuck is that on the patio door?"

It was a khaki box about six inches long and four inches tall, affixed to the glass with four transparent rubber suckers. On the bottom was a clear plastic tray split into three compartments, each filled with a centimetre of water.

"Craig drank half a case of beer and decided it would be a phenomenal idea to spend twenty-three pounds on a bird feeder. It's like having Kensington Palace stuck to the fucking window."

"Are you slagging off my feeder? I loved giving those suckers a lick, you know." He stuck his tongue out and flicked it up and down. "Ooh look at me, I'm a lesbian."

"You're a filthy toad." Lauren laughed and punched his arm. "Anyway, I'm not."

Craig eyed her suspiciously. "Whatever you say, Lauren... anyway, please take a glass of cava from the side of the kitchen. You'll note that it isn't prosecco because in this house we are not basic. Cava is superior. In the pecking order of wines it is firstly champagne, then cremant, cava and at the bottom is prosecco and I won't hear a word otherwise. So please raise your glasses to our tidy new garden, the sun, and the ability to get drunk in an outside space without being questioned by the police for drinking in public parks."

"To the Chef and Kensal's friendly neighbourhood lesbian," Kirsten cheered.

"Thank you." Sophie bowed dramatically. "Now if you wouldn't mind buggering off into the garden, I've got a lot to do in the kitchen so you're fed before you're pissed."

The afternoon bled into the night as a French Blue sky slowly paled and allowed the sun to retire for the day. It passed without anybody pausing to notice the sky darken, the air cool and the neighbouring gatherings fall silent. Craig and Kirsten had negotiated the manoeuvre of the chunky brown sofas onto the decking outside, and only at the moment where he dropped it on his toe and swore profusely did Sophie notice the absence of Sarah, Maria and Lauren.

There was a reason she was anxious about meeting Sophie's friends, and Sophie knew it, even if Sarah never explicitly said what it was. It was happening now, right this second. When Lauren waltzed into the room, Sarah knew it was Lauren because she was exactly as Sophie had described. The Essex accent was as unmistakable as her brassy confidence as she immediately made a move to inspect the woman she had heard so much about.

Maria, with the intensely dark eyes, rounded cheeks and pointed chin, regarded Sarah with some suspicion too. Kirsten had a kinder expression, a slight tan and freckled nose, and did not fill Sarah with the anxiety that Maria and Lauren did.

After some persuasion and the proclivity for sharing confidences, they had naturally negotiated a talk between them in Sophie's bedroom. She loved Sophie. She had to show them just how much and make them understand.

Sarah assumed they knew everything, and they did, though there was a huge part of her that wished they didn't, wished they didn't know that about her before meeting her. But she could only blame herself; perhaps if she'd had the courage to meet them before, they could have made their minds up for themselves.

Changing their minds didn't seem so unrealistic a prospect once they began to talk. They were worried, of course they were, and they said as much very emphatically. And it was reassuring in many senses.

"She loves you, I've never seen her this mad for somebody," Lauren had said and smiled as she did so. She didn't hate her, or if she did, she hid it well.

"But you can't just keep going by yourself. I get what it's like, you think coming out to Spanish Catholics is easy?" Maria said. "I couldn't have done it alone. But when you love somebody... you find a way."

"Kirsten?" Sarah asked.

"Not at the time, we met much later."

"Did... did your family... how did your family–?" Sarah said incoherently.

"Not well, at first. I didn't look how they'd expect a lesbian to look. I still had the long hair and the painted fingernails and they were convinced I just hadn't found the right man yet," Maria said. "And then they came around to it. I do have a few cousins that don't speak to me but I don't see them, I never really did so I don't care."

"Oh I couldn't, my cousins..."

"How many of them do you have?" Lauren asked.

"Eighty-seven," Sarah replied in a heartbeat and smiled as Lauren's eyes widened in shock.

"And you would rather be on speaking terms with every single of those eighty-whatever cousins than be happy with the love of your life?"

Sarah was stumped.

Of course she wanted to be happy with Sophie, and to tell everybody. But she couldn't come to terms with being the source of family gossip and tension. Maria had a point though; she had five cousins all called Barry and two of them had the same surname too. And when did she see them? Five years ago at Caroline's wedding. One of them was so drunk he couldn't remember his name. And she was concerned about their opinions?

"They really care about you, you know." Warm arms snaked around Sophie's waist and lips damp with wine placed a kiss between her bare shoulder blades. "Don't keep cooking, come outside."

"Where did you disappear to? I thought they'd kidnapped you and locked you in the cupboard under the stairs." Sophie smiled as Sarah came to rest in the side of her body as she stirred a pot of soup.

"Don't you think you've cooked enough? Come on, outside." Sarah whispered, running a hand down Sophie's back until it came to rest on her bum.

"I'm curious now, what did they say? You don't seem..." Sophie couldn't find the right word. *Scared? Upset? Anxious?* She had been on the end of a Maria/Lauren interrogation before and she didn't fare too well.

"Just that you don't expect to be coming home with me, yet you just want to know there's light at the end of the tunnel and you aren't wasting time fighting a losing battle." Sarah kissed her on the shoulder. "I'm sorry, I didn't realise how important it was to meet your friends."

"Thank you." Sophie bowed her head to kiss waiting lips. You couldn't buy friends like hers.

"You two, stop being gross," Lauren shouted into the flat. "Soph, do you still have that box of cigars on top of the cupboard?"

"Christ, she's turned into Del Boy," Sophie muttered and opened the doors.

Sophie stood on the threshold of the flat and the decking watching Sarah, Craig and Lauren huddled together in enthusiastic conversation. Sarah was all smiles with a glass in one hand and a cigarette in the other, wildly gesticulating with both in the middle of a story.

Lauren sat with one leg cocked on the raised flowerbed, her elbow resting on her knee. In her hand she held a chunky cigar which she smoked like Winston Churchill.

Maria and Kirsten were wrapped up on the sofa, the bright embers of a dying fire casting a warm orange glow over their softly smiling faces under a vast night sky speckled with stars. Sophie's two worlds had finally melted together, bound by earnest apologies and well-intentioned promises.

Chapter Twenty-Six

"You have excelled yourself, my darling. That was delicious." Sarah sat back against the headboard and placed her empty bowl on the bedside shelf.

"One of my favourite hobbies is eating in bed," Sophie replied with a mouthful of risotto, paying no attention to the woman beside her who sat smirking with a cocked eyebrow.

Sarah resumed the rapid tapping on her keyboard. It was nine p.m. on a Sunday and she was determined to get ahead on the emails which had been racking up slowly over the weekend. She really had not been on form last week and had let it get on top of her. The voices on her phone became more agitated as the week wore on and their emails went unanswered.

This week was going to be different. It was going to be very different. The first thing on Monday morning she was going to ring the clinic and book in for a counselling consultation which she would continue and had promised to go weekly. She was going to start preparing for the rest of her life, a life she so dearly wanted Sophie to be a part of.

Her boss, Matthew, had been on the phone a couple of times to check whether she was all right. "Your emails are a little short recently, are you OK?" he'd asked.

Illness; she blamed it on illness and not feeling herself, which wasn't the huge lie it could have been.

"Well, I've got a proposition for you," he'd started, then made a joke that she needn't worry because it was nothing she'd need to report him to HR for. It was a job. A new position, effectively a promotion. It was brilliant news; she was thrilled to be even considered for the role. She hadn't applied yet, but God she wanted to.

The only snag was that it was back in Ireland. She'd be based in Dublin and leading on the development of a new complex, a luxury retail portfolio of restaurants, shops and apartments. The opportunity was fantastic; she could leave behind a job she liked, working with men who were clinging on for their pension who didn't like answering to a woman in property, to lead a team of people-like-her, where they'd be on the ground and she'd be in charge.

But it was in Ireland. And Sophie wasn't in Ireland. But... Sophie could be in Ireland. Well, she'd said so much while they were on the river.

Sure, there wouldn't be marriage and kids on the horizon any time soon, not at all, but it was a step. A certain step closer to the future they wanted.

"Sophie?" Sarah looked up from her screen and relaxed her face; the eyebrows she pushed together in concentration softened, as did the dimples on her chin from her tightly pursed lips. "I don't know how to say this, so I'm just going to come right out and say it."

Sophie whipped her head up from her book so quickly she heard her neck crack.

"No, no, no, it's not bad, I promise," Sarah assured her to get ahead of the thoughts which she could see whirring through her head. "There's just been a vacancy announced in my company. My boss thinks I'd be... really great at it."

"That's amazing. Are you going for it?" Sophie grinned and reached for her hand.

"I want to... but it's in Ireland. And well, if I got it, I'd have to go back..."

"Okay..." Sophie held her breath, and her heart rate slowed until it was barely a dull thud that beat periodically.

"I was wondering... well, would you come with me?" Sarah said. "To Ireland, I mean. Would you move to Ireland with me?"

Sophie's body relaxed. "I mean, yes, of course. You know I'd support you."

"To be honest, I thought about applying and not saying anything until I knew they were interested in me but you know, there's a very good chance I won't get it, But if I did, it would be amazing. And it would be even more amazing if you were there with me." Sarah looked at her with hopeful eyes and a soft smile. She raised Sophie's hand to kiss it gently.

"I'm with you all the way."

"We'd have to find you a job."

"Why? I was thinking I'd be a kept woman," Sophie ribbed, smiling as she watched Sarah pull a myriad of faces, not knowing how to react. "I'm kidding. I can work anywhere. I'm assuming you have restaurants in Ireland, right?"

Behind a heavy black door flanked by tall columns and topped with a cream portico, 77 Dover Street was ready for action. Almost. Hector was AWOL after deciding he hated his suit and suddenly finding a new one became more important than the opening of his newest restaurant.

Sophie's fringe stood vertically, like a peacock fanning its feathers, from the number of times she'd pushed her fingers back through her scalp in anxiety and frustration.

"Drink this," Ana had said, marching up to her with an amber-coloured liquid on a silver tray which she downed in one with no question and shuddered.

"What was that?"

"Medicinal," she said

It had been decided by Hector, with little room for discussion to the contrary, that the canapés should be served not by waiters but actors, each dressed as a character from Greek mythology. Though what relevance Greek mythology had to the Andalusian cuisine 77 Dover Street was hoping to be famous for, she had no idea.

For days Hector had holed up in his glass-fronted office nursing a copy of *Mythos* by Stephen Fry on his lap as if he had given birth to it, painstakingly copying out his favourite excerpts onto A3 paper. The following week, he carried forty yards of varying fabrics, piled so high in his arms his bald head was barely visible, into his office with a pair of scissors and created a three-day nightmare for the cleaners. When his vision had been clearly articulated on the walls, he was ready to begin casting.

"Casting? What am I supposed to ask for?" Ana's jaw dropped and she gestured at the sheet of paper with a sketch of a round-faced man with a metal mask around his head, supposedly Hephaestus the God of Metalwork. "Give me a young Danny DeVito dressed as a horny steel gimp?"

Sophie almost spat out her coffee as Ares strode over the marble floor in red leather sleeves trimmed with iron, two metal straps crisscrossing his muscular torso down to a pleated kilt and knee-high sandals. *Christ almighty*, Sophie thought.

Ornate and original Georgian coving had been expensively restored, a custom ceiling piece had been carved and inlaid with gold leaf around the ceiling roses. The only splashes of colour would have been navy velvet banquettes and midnight napkins set atop crisp linen tablecloths; that was, if Hector hadn't continued with the Greek theme and insisted on importing olive trees and roses were sprayed with gold.

It was a small concession, she thought, given the list had originally included having the floor cleared of tables for a small-scale arena where he could stage a gladiator fight.

Names Sophie recognised from the Sidebar of Shame littered the guest list like confetti. They would turn up for the photographers stationed at the door, pose for a photo, take a drink, eat a canapé, walk once around the venue and leave again for the next scheduled stop.

It would be Hector, the man of the night, entertaining them. He would sit in the corner of the room like Santa in his grotto, with a bottle of Dom on ice, as they came to pay homage. He would have them believe that he devised the concept, seduced the chef into working for him, wrote the menu, sourced the finest suppliers, sourced investor funding and designed the space all by himself.

Sophie set her laptop down on the oak-trimmed bar with garlands wound down the silver poles. Producers in black T-shirts and headsets carried in seven-foot-tall trees and perilously perched on the top of ladders to pin flowers to the picture rails.

They were nowhere near being finished.

Electricians strode from one side of the room to the other in their blue overalls with tools strewn at various points over the floor. A plumber had moved forward the glasswasher and a pipe had burst behind the bar. Sophie rushed from the office to inspect the damage. Dirty marks had been scratched into the marble and made Sophie wince, given how much per square foot they had paid for it.

"Nasty mark, isn't it?" said a lanky man with prominent cheekbones and sandy hair, who had appeared at the other side of the bar and offered his hand. "Hi, I'm Nicholas."

He moved to perch on the silver and blue bar stool and order a cappuccino from the sommelier, who regarded the strange man with a raised eyebrow and summoned the barista from the kitchen.

"Hello," she said to the stranger, a well-spoken man who would have made many a young girl weak-kneed with his Chelsea charm.

"I hope the weather keeps for tonight." He smiled disarmingly.

"Ah, yes. So do I. There's nobody harder to entertain than drenched celebrities," she said, hoping he'd tell her who exactly he was and why he was walking unaccompanied around the restaurant so unfinished.

"I'm not sure how much you know about tonight..." he started, picking up a pile of papers from the counter which she knew to be her financial forecasts for the next year, and shuffling them on his knee before setting them back, "but we have fourteen key actors dressed as different gods from Greek mythology serving ten different canapés to guests, they'll come out from about nine-thirty-"

"Nine p.m." Sophie interrupted. She gave him a pointed smile. "And there will be twenty gods."

Nicholas looked at her quizzically, confused by the paradoxical shift in dynamic that had occurred between them. He was not being condescending; he was just being thoughtful, helpful even, to the woman who had walked in looking flustered and red-faced.

"You're...?"

"In charge," Sophie said. "And you are?"

"Oh," he said. "I'm doing a work placement at H.E.R. Events."

"Well, Nicholas, it's been lovely to meet you but I do have to work on sorting this burst pipe before I have three hundred guests arriving at a restaurant that's currently still under construction."

She smiled tightly. *Bloody work experience kids,* she thought.

"So, I've turned the water off at the mains so we won't flood the place but we're going to have to do an emergency parts run..." said Norman as he emerged from the basement and placed his oily hands on the pristine plaster.

Sophie winced. They had a lot of work to do.

"Eupheme, we can see your nipples through the linen. Please can you see if there are any pasties in the dressing room?" asked Sophie. She was primped, she was ready, she had driven a rental car with a dodgy clutch to Wembley and back wearing nude heels which hurt like hell, to retrieve nuts, bolts and other plumbing parts she couldn't name.

But the glasswasher had been fixed, it was working, she was happy, the team were happy, and Hector had just turned up dressed head to toe in fuchsia velvet and round blue glasses. He never wore glasses. Sophie didn't have time to question; she was short of two imps and a tray of canapés had vanished.

Fake Doric columns wrapped with warped golden stems, which twisted and turned around each other, punctuated the restaurant brimming with names both known and unknown. Four Muses, their lavender tulle togas draped around lithe bodies, greeted guests at the door with trays of champagne, their names ticked off a heavily vetted list.

They had built a pergola around the bar. The highest peak of the dome barely missed the high ceilings and had caused Sophie a near heart attack as the builders almost took down the ceiling rose.

In the corner of the room stood a portly man with tufts of white hair protruding from his ears wearing a suit from Savile Row. He had pearly beads of moisture gathering around his hairline and a face like a melted welly. She recognised his face but could not place his name.

The glamorous crowd glittered with a faint sheen of sweat and tugged at their shirt collars, begging for a non-existent breeze to whisk down their backs. The doors to the cocktail garden at the rear had been wrenched open and people jostled and clamoured to grab a space.

Sophie had negotiated with Westminster Council for months to secure planning permission for a small terrace within the yard which came with the plot. She was pleased with the outcome – eventually. Terracotta pots glazed blue and yellow towered with plants which toppled down the sides. She'd had the walls painted and decorated with ceramic plated mirrors to reflect the light and make the measly space feel bigger than it was.

"It's hotter than Satan's arsehole in here," Sophie muttered. "Michael, please can you turn up the air con?"

Jewels of sweat crashed down Sarah's forehead; the thick humidity was almost suffocating. The azure sky was smattered with cotton clouds drifting casually by, not once offering a brief respite from the heat of the sun which shone with intensity of a thousand more.

Dry ice flowed down pale stone steps like a dreamy mist in a cool spring morning. At the foot stood a photographer hovering too close for comfort, jumping enthusiastically at each opportunity.

"I wish that woman would fuck off already," Lauren hissed in her ear.

"You can go in now," said the nymph at the door.

They walked through the heavy curtains holding the heat from the air-conditioned room. The drastic shift in temperature orchestrated a collective sigh of relief from those who walked through. Sarah's heart was in her mouth as her amber eyes scanned the crowd for familiar faces and came up blank. She too breathed a sigh of relief for a different reason.

Under a faux-stone dome covered in magnolia, which tickled the heads of those stood underneath, she saw Sophie chatting to a rounded man with a red face and moustache. It so happened that the rotund gentleman was a friend of Gennaro's.

The chatter of the guests wove like the breeze through brightly-coloured bodies dressed in crepe and chiffon. Through tall windows, the sky had started to turn the palest of blues against lights strung through black iron railings.

"Excuse me," Sarah watched Sophie say to the man. She strode over, wearing a knee-length fitted burgundy dress.

"You look magnificent." Sarah hummed in her ear and kissed her cheek. "Sorry we're a little late. We caught a cab in the end, couldn't face the Tube. How's it going?"

"Well, thanks. I've had to have sixteen more crates of champagne brought over brought over from the Kensington site so hoping I don't run out."

"The place looks amazing, Soph, honestly. Fat H better give you a raise after this." Lauren nudged her and winked. "Speaking of a drink, I'm off in search of one. Good job I took a hay fever tablet before turning up, eh? It's like a gangbang in a florist."

"Thank you for coming," Sophie said, placing her hand discreetly on the small of Sarah's back. Sarah didn't tense, or stiffen, at the touch. It was nice. Both of them there, together, like a real couple. Well, they were a real couple and technically this didn't make them any more so, but there was something particularly validating about having Sarah show up and prove her existence.

"Sophie…" A familiar voice carried over the crowd. She turned as Gennaro, his wavy black hair with flecks of grey at the temples pushed away from his olive face, waltzed through the crowds and towards them.

"Hello, stranger, lovely to see you here." She smiled.

"I couldn't resist coming to see what magic you had created for that man." (Gennaro said 'that man' as if he'd stood in his shit as he walked through the door).

Sophie had been surreptitiously exchanging emails with Gennaro about their hypothetical plans for his hotel chain, each message a tantalising glimpse into a life she couldn't quite let go of. She hadn't given up on her Italian dream, not entirely, even as she threw herself into her relationship with Sarah.

The emails were a secret indulgence, a parallel universe where she could imagine herself strolling through sun-drenched piazzas, sipping espresso at quaint cafes, and transforming neglected villas into boutique hotels. She'd catch herself daydreaming during particularly tedious meetings with Hector, mentally redecorating crumbling Tuscan farmhouses or planning menus filled with locally-sourced delicacies.

It was harmless, she told herself, just a bit of professional networking and a creative outlet. But deep down, she knew it was more than that. It was a lifeline to a part of herself she wasn't quite ready to let go, a reminder of the Sophie who existed before Sarah, before the complications and compromises of their relationship.

"Listen," he placed his hand on the top of her back and leaned in, "I know you have a – situation, but I wanted to let you know that somebody has approached me about the Head of Marketing role. Obviously you are the best fit in my eyes, but I do need to fill the role soon. Do you think you can have an answer for me by the end of next week?"

A loud crash caught their attention, and Sophie was thankful she was able to keep Gennaro and Sarah from further conversation, should this opportunity come out into the open.

At the bar, a guest with a name not important enough for her to remember toppled over like a Jenga tower and took six replica-clay vases down with him. He lay on the floor with his kilt over his head and legs splayed to reveal his sixty-five-year-old Crown Jewels protruding from the leg of his boxers. His wife – or his girlfriend, Sophie did not know which – out of panic and embarrassment, threw her clutch bag over the offending articles and drew an 'ooooft,' from the man as the heavy missile collided with his testicles.

"Oh sweet Jesus," Sophie said, the memory forever burned into her retinas.

Chapter Twenty-Seven

Naked and hungry, Sophie crawled from their bed into the kitchen. The party ended well – her stomach lurched – but she couldn't think about that. The last thing she remembered was Lauren taking her to one side for a stern word about how she should be enjoying the fruits of her labour.

So she did. A little *too* much.

She set the kettle to boil. Eight texts from Lauren.

00:21: Lauren – I have an elephant an F a s TR guy.

00:23: Lauren – Am so drunk and confused.

00:32: Lauren – Nearly home

00:32: Lauren – Battery isiw

00:34: Lauren – Best light my life

01:08: Lauren – I feel asleep and git sick

01:09: Lauren – Can walk stalgkt

01:10: Lauren – I have an elephant

The flat was boiling. Sophie wanted to open the windows but couldn't without flashing her bits to the neighbours, so she opted for lying on the cold laminate floor and thanking God for Helen being away for the weekend.

On the coffee table was an empty bottle shaped like a skull. It had been her 'well done' present begrudgingly signed by Hector in Ana's perfect handwriting.

Beside it was Sarah's phone. Sarah was asleep in the bedroom, dead to the world since three a.m. when they had called the party off and switched Madonna off the TV.

Sarah was never without her phone; funny that she had forgotten to take it to bed with her. Sophie lay on the floor, staring at the little black box which obviously tormented her with the truth of her girlfriend. It was outrageous to think it, a major invasion of privacy and an unforgivable, psychotic thing to do.

Sophie maintained that Sarah would delete her dating profile when she was ready. But the notifications were still there, sometimes. Less frequently, admittedly, but their presence irked her no end. Even as recently as last week a little red badge had appeared while they watched a video in bed, quickly flicked away as if nothing had ever interrupted, but she remembered it clearer than what they were watching.

It was there for the sake of appearances, Sarah said, not in so many words. It was easier to have the conversation half-heartedly about dating than it was to explain to Aoife and Morag why she had seemingly given up on men, and love.

Yet not knowing had started to worm its way into her conscience, a small voice fanning the flames of burgeoning insecurity. To breach Sarah's privacy was unforgivable. She loved her, that's what mattered. She adored the bones of her. Sarah was going to counselling, she was going to Manchester with her for their year anniversary the month following and planned on meeting her parents; she wouldn't hurt her. But, powered by her curiosity and need to silence the voices in her head, Sophie reached out to the coffee table and unlocked the device.

She could hear the uninterrupted snoring from the other room, yet she still stopped. What would happen if she didn't like what she found? Surely, there was nothing even to find. She was sick with guilt though that didn't stop her scrolling straight to the screen with that icon and clicking it to find out for herself.

Today of all days, the application refreshed itself. *Fuck, hurry up,* Sophie willed. The duvet rustled, and she jumped. Eager eyes scanned the list of notifications... the messages from before Christmas, they didn't count, the ones after Christmas had been ignored, unread. *Phew.* Apart from... one.

She clicked it.

'Hi Sarah, how're you tonight?' from an inoffensive-looking man called Adam.

To which she had replied 'Hi Adam, I'm good thanks, how are you?'

There were no other messages. It was a dead conversation and there was nothing there that should have irked her, apart from the date it was sent. May 26th.

Sophie checked her calendar. They weren't together that night, nor was Sarah in Ireland or away with work. That meant she was there in the flat, left to her own devices, and he took her fancy enough in that moment for her to reply to him. What would she have said if he messaged again? Would she carry on the conversation? Would she tell Sophie? How much further would it have gone?

So much for keeping the app for the sake of appearances.

She was crushed, but she only had herself to blame for snooping in places she did not belong. A mixture of disappointment and shame fought for her attention with equal effort. There was no way she could address it without revealing what she'd done, like a petulant child who wanted to eat the sweets she'd known would make her sick.

"Sophie, can you see my phone in there?" a sleepy voice called from the bedroom.

"Y-yes. I'll ... er... bring it through."

"Oh, you're mighty," Sarah said quietly, her voice thick with sleep as she rolled over slowly to reach for her phone. Sophie busied herself with placing a cup of tea on the bedside and climbing in beside her. Sarah sat up and smiled, leaning over for a gentle kiss.

"Thank you for my tea," Sarah whispered and pulled Sophie close. The sky was grey and miserable, and so was Sophie.

"Ahh, come on now, Sarah, can you believe it? We're in the final!" Aoife cheered down the phone, her voice brimming with excitement. "This isn't any old game, it's the All-Ireland and we're in with a chance of winning."

"Ah, I can't believe it, you know," Sarah said, mouthing a thank-you to her colleague Niamh, as she passed her drink over. She already knew how the conversation would go from here.

"Are you coming home then, or what?" Aoife paused, barely giving Sarah a chance to respond before barrelling on. "Actually, never mind, Morag here isn't taking no for an answer and she's booked you a ticket leaving next Saturday afternoon."

"No, you're joking!" Sarah's mouth hung open, her mind racing through the implications. "I said I can't, I've got plans."

"And what plans are more important than this historic occasion?" Aoife demanded, her tone brooking no argument.

Well, her anniversary for one, Sarah thought. Sophie would go spare. She was supposed to be going back to Manchester to meet Sophie's parents.

Fuck. She was in trouble.

She should come clean. She should say, 'Thank you for the flights, I'll send you the money but I've been in a relationship for a year and it's our anniversary.' But the words stuck in her throat, refusing to come out.

Sarah sighed, the weight of her predicament pressing down on her. "I'm just going to take this outside," she whispered to Niamh and negotiated her way to the street. The White Horse was rammed with burly blokes in their country shirts with their arms around each other, grinning from ear to ear.

"Ah, Sarah, cop on to yourself now. It'll be a laugh! I know a man who knows a man who could get us a few tickets," Aoife said, her enthusiasm undiminished by Sarah's hesitation.

"Sure, now, Aoife. Every man and his dog will be after a pair of those. They're like rocking-horse shit," Sarah replied. "I'll send you the money for the flights, but I am not committing to coming."

"Oh, sure you are, you always go mad for the match."

It was either Aoife or Morag who disconnected the line and didn't leave room for further discussion.

Sarah stared at her phone, the blank, empty box on the weathered wooden table spattered with puddles of beer. Silver clouds bolstered their own ranks and crept over the sun until the small patches of blue almost disappeared entirely.

Despite the moral conundrum of what she was going to do next, there was nothing that could dampen the thrill of her county being in the final. It was such a big deal, a rare event that stirred something primal in her soul. She could imagine everybody in the pubs back home going absolutely mental. What she wouldn't give to be there now, with them! The familiar faces, the shared history, the electric atmosphere of anticipation – it all called to her like a siren's song.

Her mind raced with vivid images: the packed pubs with their floors sticky from spilled beer, the roar of the crowd as the teams took the field, the sea of county colours swaying in unison. She could almost taste the tang of anticipation in the air, hear the lilting accents raised in passionate debate about team selections and strategies.

But even as her heart swelled with excitement, a nagging voice in the back of her mind reminded her of Sophie, of their plans, of the promises made. The weight of her double life pressed down on her, the constant juggling act between her Irish roots and her London life suddenly feeling impossibly heavy.

Sarah's fingers hovered over her phone, torn between texting the girls and saying 'no' and calling Sophie to explain. The decision loomed before her, a crossroads that felt monumental. Whatever choice she made, she knew, would have far-reaching consequences.

You have one new email.

Subject: Your Flight Reservation RAF953 from Stansted to Dublin on 10th September

Well, there was nothing that would stop her buying a second ticket and taking Sophie with her. Oh, the match would be fantastic, and nothing would top the feeling of being in Dublin to watch it regardless of where they were.

She'd take Sophie to Brown Thomas, and then down Grafton Street for some shopping. They'd have to book a hotel. Maybe the little boutique one near The Temple. The lovely one... oh, the name would come to her. She'd ask Morag, Morag would know. Sarah's mind raced with possibilities, imagining Sophie's wide-eyed wonder at experiencing Dublin for the first time.

Sophie would love it. She wouldn't have a fucking clue what was going on during the match, but the thought of Sophie cheering alongside her, caught up in the electric atmosphere, brought a smile to Sarah's face. She'd love being there, in the middle of it all, with Sarah and her friends.

Her friends.

Yes, she'd need to tell them. The smile faltered slightly as reality set in. But then, a new thought occurred to her: she could just say Sophie was a friend from work. It was perfect, really. No need for big revelations or uncomfortable conversations. Just a simple, 'This is Sophie, we work together in London.' The tension in Sarah's shoulders eased a bit.

But even as she considered this easy way out, a part of her rebelled. They'd love Sophie if they knew the truth. Sure, they'd be a little shocked at first. They'd have had a week to come to terms with the idea. *Sarah is in a relationship, great. It's with a woman... interesting. It's with a much younger woman...* 'Sarah, you sly dog!' she could hear Aoife say. Sarah smiled.

It would be just like Aoife to give her a ribbing. Morag might be a little more surprised, a little more sceptical perhaps. That was just like her, always the careful one. Aoife once lobbed a cream bun at her own Mam's car in front of them and Morag couldn't sleep so went around to clean it off before she could notice. How they'd laughed, three fifteen-year-olds on the stone wall by the bus stop, at the thought of Morag creeping down the country lane at the dead of night like the Bleach Ninja.

She could pick up the phone right that moment and saying, 'Actually, girls, I'm not coming home alone.' She wanted to. Her fingers hovered above the screen, willing them to bite the bullet without letting thoughts linger and impose their alternative opinions about why she shouldn't.

Then, almost before she'd had the chance to:

15:57 – Aoife: You'll never guess what! We've got three tickets to Croagh Park courtesy of a fella who Morag gave a blowie to in Kehoes.

15:58 – Sarah: The one from February? Dirty bitch but good on her.

They'd be there the Friday afternoon and she'd be there the Saturday morning too. *It's better than nothing,* she thought, trying to convince herself that this compromise was enough. But deep down, Sarah knew she was treading on thin ice.

They'd fought almost immediately after Sarah told her.

The conversation started pleasantly enough. In hindsight she hadn't gone about it in the right way. She *told* Sophie what the new plan was rather than explaining why it had changed first. That got Sophie's back up and she'd almost hit the roof.

"Oh, don't be like that. I'll still be there..." Sarah rationalised, her voice taking on a placating tone that only seemed to fuel Sophie's anger. "I'll just have to go Saturday afternoon because the match isn't until Sunday."

Sophie didn't say anything but she could sense her seething.

"Sophie, please don't be mad with me. We're in the final, I don't think you understand what a big deal this is – I mean – we could win. I'll still be there," said Sarah, her words tumbling out in a desperate attempt to make Sophie understand.

"And I don't think you quite understand," came a measured voice, each word carefully enunciated as if Sophie was holding back a torrent of emotion, "that my parents have wanted to meet you for a year, only for you to leave halfway through the weekend for a football match, and on the day we had planned just for us."

Hold on a fecking minute here, Sarah thought. *No, I'm not having this. This is a big deal. This is a huge deal.* It was only fair that Morag and Aoife would expect her to go home to watch it with them. And sure, there would be twenty or so people waiting for her to get off the aeroplane and waltz on home to celebrate.

"No, I'm not happy about this. You don't understand the culture of this, this is the All-Ireland – everybody goes absolutely mental about this. I don't appreciate how you're just totally disregarding it!" Sarah gripped the edges of the table until her knuckles turned white. She glanced through the windows and into the crowded bar and saw Niamh too engrossed in conversation with a lad in a white-and-green-striped shirt to take any notice about where she had buggered off to.

"Sarah. I understand that in the eyes of your family and friends you have no real reason not to be there, because they have no idea you're even in a relationship. So how about you don't even bother coming at all and piss off back to Ireland?" Sophie barked.

"Ah, you're some tulip, Sophie!" Sarah snapped back.

Sophie hung up the phone. The abrupt end to the call left Sarah reeling, her emotions a maelstrom of anger, guilt, and frustration.

But fuck this, fuck her, fuck everything, Sarah fumed and marched back into the pub. She felt torn between two worlds, neither of which seemed to fully understand her. The excitement of the match still buzzed in her veins, but now it was tainted with the bitter taste of her fight with Sophie.

Chapter Twenty-Eight

Under the amber glow of streetlamps, they hunched under their umbrellas with high-collared coats and scarves covering stony faces, Sophie and Sarah marched down the street.

Heels clicked eagerly onto wet pavements which reflected the light shining from the windows of late-night barbers and off-licences. Putney was still buzzing with life,

Their summer had slipped away as uneventfully as their anniversary, a milestone that now felt like a distant memory rather than a celebration.

There had been no mention since of meeting Sophie's parents, as if it was a mutually accepted fact that it wasn't going to happen. Their silence on the subject spoke volumes, a tacit acknowledgment of the growing distance between them.

Sophie had placed so much importance on them meeting. It was a fresh chance for her family to see Sarah for the woman she fell in love with, not the woman they believed her to be through second- and third-hand stories.

A cautionary tale, perhaps, against divulging your secrets to even the most loving ears. Sophie wondered if she'd been naïve in sharing so much.

Their relationship was fractious, though neither dared acknowledge that aloud. Their recent evenings together now felt born out of duty rather than desire. Two women staring at different sides of the same laptop, both harbouring swathes of frustration and angst, Sarah's face lit by nothing but the blue glow from her screen until it was shut to the world and so were their eyes.

Each day passed in a haze of discontent. Sophie had fallen into a vacuum of complacency. She was fatter, paler and had a perpetual air of sadness which hung about her like a storm cloud wanting to clear the air. The changes were not just physical; she felt diminished, as if pieces of herself were slowly eroding away.

Since that fateful argument on their anniversary, their relationship had been like a slowly sinking ship, taking on water bit by bit. She remembered the stilted conversations, the half-smiles, the way Sarah's eyes would dart away when topics veered too close to their future. The silences had grown longer, their touches less frequent, until they felt like strangers sharing a bed.

Sophie recalled the nights she'd lain awake, listening to Sarah's even breathing, wondering how they'd drifted so far apart. There were moments of warmth, fleeting instances where it felt like old times, but they were quickly overshadowed by the looming reality of their situation. Sarah's reluctance to involve herself too deeply in Sophie's life had morphed from a minor irritation to a gaping wound, festering with each passing day.

Each step towards Wandsworth felt like a step away from the life they'd imagined together, and Sophie couldn't help but wonder if Sarah was thinking the same thing. The silence stretched on, broken only by the occasional passing car or distant laughter from a pub, sounds of a world that seemed increasingly separate from their own.

Sophie realised now that every unanswered text, every cancelled plan, every avoided conversation about their future had been another nail in the coffin of their relationship. The breakdown hadn't been sudden or dramatic; it had been a gradual erosion of trust and hope, leaving them both exhausted and hollow.

As they walked, Sophie couldn't help but wonder if Sarah felt the same sense of loss, the same creeping dissatisfaction. The city bustled around them, full of life and possibility, yet they seemed trapped in their own bubble of stagnation. The question 'Where do we go from here?' echoed in Sophie's mind, growing louder with each step, demanding an answer she knew she was finally ready to give.

That night they lay in bed, engulfed in the darkness, the silence that settled in the space between them almost suffocating. Sophie could hear Sarah's breathing, slightly uneven, betraying her. She wondered if Sarah knew she was awake too, if she could sense the tension radiating from her body.

The email confirmation from Alitalia sat heavy in her inbox, her flight to Florence booked for six weeks' time. After months of hesitation, she'd finally accepted Gennaro's offer.

A promotion, a fresh start, and an escape all wrapped up in one neat package. "Expect me on the 29th October." she'd written that morning, the words feeling both liberating and final. Her hands had shaken as she'd typed them but she knew it was time.

This was her commitment to herself, putting her needs first. This time would be different. She wouldn't let Sarah's tears or promises change her mind.

Gennaro had an apartment arranged, a beautiful third-floor walk-up in Santa Croce with a tiny balcony overlooking a bustling piazza. Gennaro had even connected her with his sister who taught English at the university, promising Sophie wouldn't feel alone. The opportunity career-defining and this was her dream, but most importantly, it was three countries and a two-and-a-half-hour flight away from London – and Sarah.

Sophie was on the verge of turning over, of breaking the silence herself, when Sarah's voice cut through the darkness, low and hesitant.

"Sophie?" Sarah whispered, her voice barely audible. "Are you awake?"

Sophie's heart raced. She took a deep breath, steeling herself for the conversation they'd been avoiding for so long.

"Come here to me, my love." A warm hand reached for her shoulder so that she might lie and face her lover. Sophie turned, facing Sarah in the dim light of dawn. She could make out the contours of Sarah's face, the worry lines etched around her eyes, the slight tremble of her lips.

The sun was rising rapidly and London awoke with the steady rumble of passing cars and screeching of children as they rocketed down the pavements in a flurry of pink, purple, green and blue coats.

"I can't give you what you want," Sarah whispered with tears clamouring behind her eyes, a hand covering Sophie's cheek. "But I can't lose you. I need you."

The words hung heavy between them, a confession and a plea rolled into one. Sophie felt a surge of emotions – frustration, love, disappointment – all warring within her. It felt like a relief, though the darkness offered little comfort to either of them. What a strange feeling it was, to dissect her relationship when the urge to fight for it had long since dissolved.

"No, no you don't," Sophie replied softly. "But I'll tell you what I need. I need to be your first consideration, not your last. I need you to care about my opinion more than those of people who do not care much for yours."

Sarah sniffed and wiped her face with a clammy hand. Sophie took it and held it tightly in her own.

"You know, I never wanted you to dance around Cork with a rainbow flag around your neck claiming to be a flaming homosexual," said Sophie. "I just want to be accepted. And that's fair, isn't it? Nobody else's opinion should matter. You should be able to love me unselfconsciously, but let's be realistic, I don't think that's possible."

The Irishwoman began to shake. Tears ran across the bridge of her nose and down her cheeks to create a small dark patch on the lilac pillowcase. Sophie watched, her heart breaking even as she knew this was necessary.

"I've never loved anybody as much as I love you, Sophie, you're my girlfriend and you're my best friend," she replied through her tears, two hands clasped tightly in her clammy embrace. "This is a completely different kind of love to what I've ever had before. It's so pure, and you love all of me despite my faults. But I'm not sure what kind of love this is. I don't know if it's love for a friend or somebody who I want to spend the rest of my life with. But my family, my... my friends, they – they won't accept this. They won't accept us. And I can't bring more shame to them, I just, I can't."

Suddenly Ireland felt so far away after all. She wanted to hear her Mam's mundane chatter at the end of the phone about what Edith from Bridge Club had said when she'd had too much sherry, or hear Caro telling her what Charlie had been doing at nursery. Fiona welcomed the first girl into the family only months ago. She missed them, she missed them all so much.

She'd move home at some point, England wasn't her forever place. She'd mentioned it once to Sophie, casually in passing – about whether she'd move with her if the opportunity arose, just to see what she'd say.

Sophie didn't even bat an eyelid, of course; she'd agreed. After all, she could work anywhere. 'And being so far from home wouldn't bother you?' Sarah had asked.

'Why would it? I'd be with you,' Sophie said as if it was the simplest thing in the world. And it was, the simplest thing, so easy to love but not seemingly to accept something you didn't think you deserved.

Sarah's words were a jumble of love and fear, hope and resignation. Sophie listened, feeling a strange sense of calm settle over her. She had known, deep down, that this moment would come.

Sarah's body shivered and sobbed. Her porcelain-white complexion turned pink with tears and her eyes clamped shut. She reached out and wrapped her arms around Sophie in an iron grip. Hot tears dropped thick and fast onto sticky, shimmering skin,

Sophie was the Tin Woman, clutching at a dry tissue, enveloped by an unnerving peace like a heaven-sent calm. She knew long ago that she had lost. She had been elated and crushed in such quick succession that it came as a surprise for her to feel nothing at all.

"I think..." Sarah began after heaving two deep breaths to steady herself. "I think that we should go on a break."

Memories of Budapest came flooding back, and the conversations that followed. On the sofa when she was going to walk away, the begging and pleading, the constant pushing and pulling and then... she'd had enough.

"Oh, Sarah." Sophie kissed the head of curls laying under her chin. "I think it's too late for that. I think this is it for us, love."

"No, no. No..." she howled, burying her face further into Sophie's neck and tensing her arms tighter.

"Sarah, for so long you've been telling me you want us to work, all the while listing excuse after excuse about why you think we can't." Sophie's voice began to break. "Do you understand how that makes me feel? I've felt too pathetic for too long."

One tear crawled the short distance between her eyes and the duvet. *It was the right thing to do,* she said to herself. There was no coming back from where they were. Perhaps in a different time, in a different place, they could have walked a different path.

"Do you remember the job in Dublin you spoke to me about?"

Sarah nodded.

"I've been offered one in Italy. There's a chain of hotels – the owner came to the launch of one of our restaurants last year – and we kept in touch. He wanted me to take charge of their marketing and I'm going to take the job."

"Sophie..." Sarah's voice cracked on her name, the sound raw and painful. She tried to speak but the words caught in her throat as the full weight of what this meant crashed over her. This wasn't just another argument, or a bump in the road, this was Sophie choosing to leave. "That sounds... amazing. I can't... I can't believe it."

Her shoulders shook with sobs, each breath more ragged than the last. The distance between them vaster than ever, and soon to be even greater as Sophie left the country entirely.

"When... when will you go?" Sarah fought to calm herself.

Sophie moved closer, basking in the last warm moments their bodies would ever be pressed together. Soft fingers brushing the tears from Sarah's cheeks.

"Six weeks." she said softly. She forced herself to maintain eye contact, watching the impact of her words register on Sarah's face. It felt cruel – but necessary. She needed to see this through to make it real for both of them.

Sarah nodded mechanically, her breath slowing. She opened her mouth to speak, closed it again, and eventually managed to whisper, "That's... that's so soon."

They breathed in time, slow calculated breaths with their eyes closed, oblivious to the frantic screeching of emergency vehicles ripping down the roads, the rhythmic thudding coming from the wound-down windows of cars revving their engines.

"I'm going to go now," Sophie whispered.

As she gently disentangled herself from Sarah's embrace, Sophie felt a mix of sadness and relief. The end had come, not with a bang but with a whimper, in the quiet of Sarah's bedroom as the world outside came to life.

She stood, gathering her strength for the steps that would take her out of this room, out of this relationship, and into an uncertain but necessary future.

Chapter Twenty-Nine

In the first few weeks without Sophie, Sarah felt as though she was walking through a thick fog, her world muted and unfamiliar. She found herself reaching for Sophie's hand in the night, only to grasp empty air, the reality of her absence hitting her anew each time.

The silence was the worst part. No more gentle humming from the kitchen as Sophie cooked, no more animated chatter about her day at work. Sarah caught herself speaking aloud at times, turning to share a thought or a joke, only to be met with the oppressive quiet of an empty room.

She threw herself into work, staying late at the office, taking on extra projects. Anything to avoid the hollow feeling that awaited her at home. Her colleagues noticed the change – the dark circles under her eyes, the forced smiles, the way she flinched when someone mentioned relationships or weekend plans.

Nights were a battleground of conflicting emotions. Relief at no longer having to navigate the complexities of their relationship warred with a bone-deep longing for Sophie's presence. She'd curl up on Sophie's side of the bed, breathing in the fading scent of her shampoo from the pillow, torn between wanting to preserve it forever and wishing it would disappear so she could stop torturing herself.

There were moments of anger too. At Sophie for giving up, at herself for not being brave enough, at the world for making it so complicated.

She'd find herself standing in front of the mirror, rehearsing all the things she should have said, all the ways she could have fought harder.

But mostly, there was guilt. It sat heavy in her chest, a constant companion. Guilt for hurting Sophie, for not being able to give her what she needed, for choosing the comfort of her closet over the love of her life. She'd catch sight of herself in shop windows and wonder if people could see it written on her face – "Here walks a coward."

Helen tried to help, inviting her out, checking in regularly. But Sarah found it hard to be around her, knowing she was the only one who knew the full story. She couldn't bear the mix of sympathy and disappointment in Helen's eyes.

As the weeks passed, Sarah began to realise the true cost of her decision. It wasn't just Sophie she had lost, but a part of herself. The Sarah who had dared to love freely, who had glimpsed a future full of possibility, was gone. In her place was a woman who felt smaller, dimmer, less alive.

One night, about a month after Sophie left, Sarah found herself in a pub, surrounded by the boisterous cheer of a football match. As her countrymen celebrated a goal, she felt utterly alone in the crowd. In that moment, watching the jubilant faces around her, Sarah understood that while she had kept her place in this world, she had lost the person who had made her feel truly at home.

She stumbled out into the cool night, tears streaming down her face, finally allowing herself to fully feel the magnitude of what she had lost.

"Look, I need a change. I need something that excites me. I need not to be living in a flat which is practically a crap home renovation, and as much as I love Craig, with a man-child," said Sophie.

Lauren leaned forward, her brow furrowed with concern. "Listen, Sophie..." she began quietly, her tone cautious, "You've just split up with Sarah. It's a big decision to make and–"

"I think it's now or never, though," Sophie said quietly.

Lauren took a sip of her wine. She looked pensive. "I feel better knowing you're not buying a rucksack, going travelling and growing dreadlocks. I've decided you can go."

"Thank you," Sophie laughed. "How gracious. Anyway, you know I'm not a rucksack kind of girl."

"But have you tried, just you know, checking it's not because you're lonely. Download an app! See who's out there, go on a date."

"You make it sound like it's an exotic safari full of mystical creatures," Sophie said wryly. "In reality it's a barren with two mating chipmunks and a three-legged gazelle. Anyway, I tried downloading one and this morning and the first message I received was pure filth. It's been so long since I've had one of those that I had to look half the words up on urbanslang.com."

Lauren burst into laughter, nearly spilling her wine.

"Then another sent me a photo of her vulva. Thirteen years of dating women and I didn't realise women did that. It wasn't pretty."

"You know, as a lesbian it concerns me to hear you say that."

"What?"

"That you don't think vulvas are attractive."

"Well, they're part of the job description aren't they. As long as they clean and functional, I don't have a problem with them. They're not aesthetically pleasing, are they? What do you want me to do? Start doing potato prints of them? Do you think dicks are attractive?"

"Ok point taken." Lauren said between mouthfuls of pasta. "Did I tell you work are paying for me to learn Korean? It'll take me seven years and I've got to practice for an hour a day. I'd get shorter in prison."

"Here, can you pass that wine?" Sophie interrupted, reaching for the bottle. She topped up their drinks, the rich red liquid sloshing dangerously close to the rim of their glasses.

Lauren continued, undeterred by Sophie's distraction. "They said they'll either pay for me to learn that or Spanish. I said, *'Hola, churros,'* and see, I'm fluent. So I got Korean. I don't get it. Mandarin is the most spoken language in the world and at least if I learn that I could go down to Mr Ping's and practice. I don't know anybody that speaks Korean. They're all asleep when I'm awake."

Sophie choked on her dinner. Sophie found herself giggling too, a warmth spreading through her chest that she hadn't felt in weeks.

As their laughter subsided, Sophie felt a flicker of something familiar – a spark of her old self, peeking through the fog of heartbreak and uncertainty. These moments came like period pains, unexpected and intense. The brief moments of respite were few and far between, but they were there.

She had been feeling as if she was living her life from a place outside her own body, a spectre hanging around watching a pasty, grown woman muddling her way half-heartedly around London, around her life, and waiting for a tidal wave of grief which never came.

There was a bright side, Sophie thought; it was about time she was presented with an opportunity to lose the Sauvignon Blanc pounds she had accumulated before her move to Italy. Her jeans were too tight and her shirts were bursting around the bosoms and she felt horrible about herself and the world around her. She was clutching at straws; *Please Lord, let there be a silver lining.*

Heartbreak had hit, or was about to, any second now, and her appetite would go and she would be skinny. *Watch out Baywatch, Sophie's on her way.*

The walk from Regent Street to Euston seemed longer each day. *It was the rain,* she decided. The weather was miserable and so was she. Glass-fronted shops radiated light in the early darkness. The throngs of people who passed in every direction with their eyes down, backs hunched and earphones in. *How did I become one of those people?* she thought. *London. That's what it does to you, selective social interaction.*

After the launch of Dover Street, Hector had taken himself on a month-long holiday. For Sophie, it was a glorious respite away from – well, away from Hector. The new site was doing well, really well; the bookings they had seen in their first week or two had plateaued in the months that followed but they were consistently booked up for weekends with a strong showing on Wednesday and Thursday night.

While the new site smashed all targets, the Notting Hill restaurant had begun to stall, through no reason she could discern. Hector went berserk, even from New Zealand. It was her fault, as usual – not the fact he launched restaurants and then left them alone so he could move onto the next. It was up to her to keep them afloat.

What was she to do, summon bookings from thin air? Persuade the landlords not to increase the rent on a prime West London site? The man was ludicrous. Gennaro would never have behaved in that manner.

Thinking of Gennaro, Sophie found herself reaching for her phone. Their conversations had become more frequent lately, a lifeline of sanity in the chaos of her professional life.

Gennaro's warm voice filled the line. "Sophie, *mia cara!* How are you?"

"Gennaro, I'm at my wits' end here," Sophie sighed, sinking into her office chair. "Hector's on the warpath about Notting Hill, and I'm running out of ideas. The sooner I'm on a plane, the better."

"Ah, the troubles of success," Gennaro chuckled. "Tell me, what's happening?"

Sophie launched into a detailed explanation of the situation, the words tumbling out in a rush. Gennaro listened patiently, occasionally humming in understanding or asking a clarifying question.

"You know," he said when she finished, "in Italy, we have a saying, *'Non tutte le ciambelle riescono col buco.' Not all doughnuts come out with a hole.* Sometimes, despite our best efforts, things don't go as planned."

"That's lovely, Gennaro, but it doesn't help me fix Notting Hill," Sophie replied, a hint of frustration in her voice.

"No, but it reminds us that not every venture will be a runaway success. The key is how we respond. Now, tell me, have you considered..."

For the next hour, they bounced ideas back and forth. Gennaro's approach was methodical, focused on understanding the root of the problem rather than just treating symptoms. It was refreshing, so different from Hector's knee-jerk reactions and blame game.

As they wrapped up the call, Gennaro said, "Sophie, you know this is all on him. It's not a reflection on you."

Sophie took herself down the street to an expensive bakery off Carnaby Street. She bought an excessively large slice of chocolate cake. As she sat in the quaint cafe, she perused restaurant recommendations in Florence during her lunch break. Hector called twice; she declined each one. He could wait to be a rampant tosser again when she sat back at her desk.

Later that evening, she got home to find their flat had been broken into, and Craig hadn't even noticed. He'd been home for an hour already. The absurdity of the situation struck her immediately.

It was odd, she thought, that there seemed to be a large chunk of plaster missing on the wall behind the door. White powder and chunks of it were clumped in a small patch on the mahogany-coloured laminate floor. There were no obvious signs of being burgled, apart from when she went to retrieve her iPad and found it had gone, alongside the ten-year-old MacBook with a broken screen it was next to.

"Craig, check the emergency fund on the bookcase in the living room," she shouted, her heart racing.

"What do you mean?" He walked into the kitchen in his underpants with a spoon of ice-cream hanging out of his mouth. "It's gone."

"Fuuuuck."

She'd almost lost her temper. Somebody forcing the door would have seen the ancient wood rocket out of its ancient door frame and against the wall. How a grown man could come home and not notice the foot-long hole in the wall, or notice but not think anything was amiss, was mind-boggling.

Sophie walked into Craig's room, surveying the chaos. "No wonder you didn't notice. They probably took one look in here and didn't want to bother. It looks like the aftermath of the Dresden bombings in here."

The police officer who visited briefly was less than reassuring. "The lock is only as good as the door frame it's in. This looks original with the house. We can't promise we'll get anywhere with this; looks like they were in and out. Nobody saw a thing."

The locksmith didn't come to fit a new lock until two a.m., his arrival announced by the angry mutterings of disturbed neighbours. That pissed off half the street. Their landlord, a man tighter than a fish's arsehole, would only pay when she threatened him with court. Craig had been as soft as a baked aubergine throughout the entire debacle.

She'd gone to work late the next day, and Hector had gone ballistic again. As she sat at her desk, feeling the weight of everything pressing down on her, Sophie realised that enough was enough. With a deep breath and a sense of resolve, she reached for her phone.

"Hector, this is the last time you're going to be a tosser to me. I'm handing my notice in and you can get fucked."

Chapter Thirty

1   11:04 – Sarah: Hey, I'm parked outside.

11:05 – Sophie: Aren't you coming in?

11:05 – Sarah: No, I don't want to bump into Craig.

Sarah sat in her car, her knuckles white as she gripped the steering wheel. Tears began to prick her eyes and sadness gathered in her chest like a weight she couldn't shift no matter how hard she tried. This was it.

The guilt had been unbearable. Helen had been amazing, the creature, the only person to know what she was going through, and an unwavering pillar of support through her teary episodes and exhausted ramblings.

The job offer in Ireland, which had once been a source of internal conflict, now beckoned like a lifeline. She accepted it, feeling a mix of trepidation and excitement as she signed the contract.

The prospect of returning home stirred something in her that had long been dormant. She began to rediscover pieces of herself that she'd tucked away during her time in London. The lilt in her accent grew stronger, as if her voice remembered its roots.

Planning her move became a form of therapy. She threw herself into finding flats in Dublin, comparing rental properties, and mapping out her new commute. Each decision felt like a step towards reclaiming her identity, towards becoming the Sarah she used to be – confident, ambitious, and unapologetically herself.

She started reaching out to old friends, rekindling connections that had faded over the years. Late-night phone calls filled with laughter and shared memories reminded her of the support system waiting for her back home.

And of course, Aoife and Morag were beside themselves that she would only be a drive away.

There were moments of doubt, of course. Times when she'd walk past a place that held memories of Sophie, and the pain would hit her anew. But increasingly, these moments were overshadowed by a growing sense of purpose and anticipation.

One evening, as she was sorting through her belongings, Sarah came across an old notebook. Flipping through it, she found a list she'd made years ago, before moving to London. It was filled with dreams and goals – things she'd wanted to achieve, places she'd wanted to go. With a start, she realised how many of those dreams she'd set aside, how much of herself she'd compromised.

Impulsively, she grabbed a pen and began adding to the list. New goals, new dreams – some big, some small, but all uniquely hers. As she wrote, she felt a familiar spark of excitement, a feeling she hadn't experienced in years.

The woman staring back at her wasn't the same one who had arrived in London years ago, bright-eyed and full of ambition. Nor was she the woman who had lost herself in a relationship, in a constant battle between desire and reality. This Sarah was someone new – shaped by her experiences, strengthened by her heartbreak, and ready to embrace a future on her own terms.

There had been a date, an optimistic attempt at distracting herself, but it was a disaster. Still, she was trying. It was a start at least.

The car door opened, and Sophie slid into the passenger seat. The familiar scent of her perfume filled the air, and Sarah's heart clenched.

Hot tears prodded her pink-rimmed eyes and she started to apologise, words spilling out between sobs. Sophie made a joke, as if they were old friends, yet they held hands like former lovers.

Sarah reached out, wrapping her arms around Sophie's neck and pulled her closer. This was familiar, it was right, it was them. It was their last.

Tears rolled from Sarah's cheeks down Sophie's neck and under the collar of her robe. They sat there, the gear stick uncomfortably prodding Sarah in the ribs, though she was unwilling to part from her former lover.

Sarah cupped Sophie's face, looking at her solemnly. "I will always love you. You know that, don't you? And nobody will ever go down on me like you did."

"I know," Sophie responded with a soft smile.

"What will you do now?" Sarah asked, realising she was the only person Sophie hadn't told about her plans.

As Sophie began to speak about her move to Italy, Sarah felt a mix of emotions. Pride in Sophie's courage, sadness at the finality of their parting, and a glimmer of hope for her own future.

"I'm going back to Ireland," Sarah blurted out, surprising herself. "I've taken that job we talked about."

Sophie's eyes widened, then softened with understanding. "That's wonderful, Sarah. You'll be brilliant."

They sat in silence for a moment, both processing the paths that were diverging before them.

"I guess this is really it, then," Sarah said, her voice cracking.

Sophie nodded, squeezing Sarah's hand. "It is. But we'll be okay. Both of us."

As Sophie stepped out of the car, Sarah felt a chapter closing. But for the first time in months, she also felt the possibility of a new one beginning. She watched Sophie walk away, then started her car, ready to drive towards her own future – back home, back to herself.

Chapter Thirty-One

The grass rippled in a roaring wind that thundered past her ears and trees with bowed branches rustled in response, their amber leaves swept into a furore which raced down the street. The air was cold and unwelcoming; it seeped into her lungs like thick fog and condensed on the hedgerows as drops of morning dew.

Her backlit shadow, reflected in the window covered with a light spray of rain, stared back at her and the bright lights of London, though so early in the morning, whizzed past in a blur. Nocturnal lights dimmed, falling to their sleep one by one as they popped down the streets. Office blocks topped with red warning lights pierced the skyline as London began to wake.

Her last days were the best of days. Hours spent cooking elaborate dishes she would never usually have had the time or inclination to make. Afternoon strolls into Notting Hill for midweek coffee at bakeries usually overcrowded on weekends with tourists or weekend brunchers discussing the merits of quinoa. Hot deep baths filled with bubbles and lit by candlelight, an Argentinian Malbec by her side and the iPad propped on the windowsill.

She was nowhere near over her relationship with Sarah. The memories of their happiness danced in her mind. There was rarely a day that passed where she did not think of the eyes that would peer up at her as warm arms wrapped around her neck, hands that would creep from one side of the bed to the other during the night.

The heaviness of her chest slowly started to lift and allow optimism to seep in.

Sophie stopped being everybody's Fixer. The cheerer-upper, the burden-bearer, the problem-solver. She started being fearlessly selfish. *And how funny,* she thought, *that this meant leaving her home of almost ten years.* A place where she had discovered and lost her sense of self, built a network of support that ebbed and flowed, had happiness and heartbreaks that had pushed her to new heights and torn her back down again. London. A place where she was both resilient and empathetic, but now her ties to that place were no more than nostalgia and idealism. If she did not leave then she feared she would be stuck forever.

There was an apartment waiting for her on Via del Casone in a sandstone and terracotta-washed building with an owl ornately carved above the double oak door. Monochrome tiles led to a courtyard of coarse evergreen grass, lined with box hedges and flanked by palms. Off the first floor, porticos overlooking the residents' private paradise were four apartments with marble floors and high white ceilings.

The shutters creaked on their hinges and swung slowly outwards to thud on the plaster walls.

"Sorry, nobody has lived here since my grandmother," Gennaro said, whipping cream sheets from covering mahogany furniture. "This is all old. I can move them so you can make it your own. You can stay as long as you like. You might find something more modern in town that is more to your liking."

The once-white ceiling rose required a lick of paint. Ageing wallpaper fell from the tops of the walls. Sun shone through the dirty windows and lit the cloud of disturbed dust that floated listlessly in the dry air.

His leather loafers had clicked on tiled floors as he strode through the apartment, revealing mahogany chests and chairs draped in paint splattered cream linen. His wife had brought with her an assortment of tasteful decorations from well-heeled friends that Sophie had been grateful for.

She spent weekends at flea markets picking up odds and sods until, finally, it was hers. And it was an entire flat to herself. No housemates leaving crumbs in the butter or socks on the floor or pots by the sink. Her mess would be hers alone – and what a glorious thought that was.

She had missed the adventure of the unknown, of planting herself in a new environment to figure out her life, herself, her loves. A new place where those with preconceptions of her did not exist.

In a Florentine apartment she would begin again. Herbs growing on the balcony under the Mediterranean blue sky. Tulle drapes dancing in front of tall open windows. Broken Italian communications with weathered faces. Weekend flea markets.

She stood with a cup of coffee in her hand, listening to the chatter of the old men sheltering under the shade of a tree – loud voices, exuberant hands, aces, spades and queens. She watched the birds darting between the trees, soaring to new heights and plummeting into evergreen leaves. The branches they clung to would soon be bare and it would be too cold to play bridge on the street. Sophie realised that the paper cuts had started to heal and her soul finally felt at peace.

Her life was slower, more considered, her outlook irrevocably changed and for the first time, she could understand how she felt.

It was the small things that bought her the most joy. Filling her cupboards with jars of ingredients she could not pronounce, buying fresh handmade pasta, driving to Tuscan vineyards, *aperitivo* for one, watching Florence bustle past.

Though those messages from Sarah, relics of everyday conversation from a time when they had loved each other so completely, still lived on her phone like remnants of another life, she did not delete them. Instead from time to time, she would open them and read them back – not from longing, but to remind herself that an all-consuming love had once existed and that one day, it would live again.

Even when her mind would wander too far, to a life that could have been but was never destined to be, she would feel a tender ache but see ever clearer why it could not exist.

And each afternoon when the alarm beeped for five o'clock, the screen of her computer fell black and the walk home began. Over the famous Florentine bridges and down the river as the sun began to set over the villas and Duomo, Sophie entered a tranquillity she had never known and a space she could finally call her own.

Sophie had found what she had longed for. Blissful days that bled graciously into the night. Dreams of happiness to inspiring waking contentedness, the most magnificent hopes and the confidence to achieve them, and the openness to stand on the brink of the unknown with her arms cast open.